Other books by Caryl Lewis

SEED

THE MAGICIAN'S DAUGHTER

Caryl Lewis

Illustrated by George Ermos

MACMILLAN CHILDREN'S BOOKS

Published 2023 by Macmillan Children's Books
an imprint of Pan Macmillan
The Smithson, 6 Briset Street, London EC1M 5NR
EU representative: Macmillan Publishers Ireland Ltd, 1st Floor,
The Liffey Trust Centre, 117–126 Sheriff Street Upper
Dublin 1, D01 YC43
Associated companies throughout the world
www.panmacmillan.com

ISBN 978-1-5290-7816-9

Text copyright © Caryl Lewis 2023
Illustrations copyright © George Ermos 2023

3 5 7 9 8 6 4 2

A CIP catalogue record for this book is available from the British Library.

Printed and bound by CPI Group (UK) Ltd, Croydon CR0 4YY

For Gwenno, Erin and Abigail.
You three are magic!

'The most beautiful experience we can have is the mysterious' – Albert Einstein

CHAPTER ONE

'Ladies and Gentlemen, Boys and Girls, what you are about to witness is a magical feat which has been a year in the making! A treat for the imagination, the likes of which has NEVER been seen at Sunny Haven Holiday Park before. A splendiferous illusion that will knock your socks off . . .'

Abby watched breathlessly through the red velvet curtains at the side of the stage, her stomach in a knot as Dad slipped his magic wand from his trouser waistband and waved it mysteriously over the box on the rickety table in front of him. Although the stage lights were blinding, Abby could still make out the sweat on her dad's forehead, the tension in his jaw and, to her left, the dozens of expectant upturned faces in the crowd. The younger kids were, as usual, sitting cross-legged on the floor in the front. Their older brothers and sisters were chewing gum and looking at their phones, and behind them were the usual frazzled mixture of sun-burned mums, dads, grandads, aunts and uncles who were hoping that the onsite entertainment would at least give them an hour's peace from their energetic families and a nice sit down.

'As you can see,' continued Dad mysteriously, picking up the box and sweeping it dramatically from side to side, 'this box is completely empty. Can you please confirm to me that it is empty?'

There was no reply, just the sound of coughing and crinkly crisp packets and the odd baby crying.

'I said, can you see that it is empty?' he asked again, louder this time, while cupping his hand behind his ear theatrically.

'Yes!' came the bedraggled response. Dad smiled and returned to the table and placed the box down again with a flourish, but Abby could tell by his breathing that he was nervous.

Ever since Little Mike, the holiday park site manager, had threatened to sack him if he didn't up his magical game. Barbara the cabaret singer had had to modernize her song choices from Songs That Won the War to chart-topping hits, the ballroom dancers had been dropped for a street dancing group and Dad, well, Dad was on thin ice. This was the first show of the season, and his last chance to impress Little Mike, who was now standing on a box in the back of the entertainment hall so he could see over the heads of the audience. His twice-dyed hair was slicked down and his suit was so sharp it could draw blood. And even in the low light, Abby could see Little Mike's over-whitened teeth shine against his tanned face, practically glowing in the dark.

Abby watched as Dad waved his magic wand over and around the box in order to show that there were no tricks or wires, that there wasn't anything suspicious going on . . . Then, when he was ready, he grabbed the box and threw it into the air before catching it again and this time, he reached into the box and pulled out Abby's white rabbit Ta-da, who blinked uncertainly in the spotlights.

There came a small ripple of clapping from the audience and the little children started laughing and pointing.

'Now!' said Dad gaining confidence, 'I'm going to make this rabbit disappear again!'

Dad stroked Ta-da before putting him back in the box and picking it up once again. Then, as he had practised, he threw it into the air. Abby heard the audience gasp as it sailed upwards as if in slow motion, before landing back in her father's hands.

This time, there was absolute silence. Some of the little ones in front had their hands over their mouths in shock. And then, with a broadening smile, Dad showed them . . . the empty box. Ta-da had disappeared!

There came some proper applause this time, and Abby could just about make out Little Mike looking pleased. Abby's shoulders relaxed as she watched Dad hit his stride.

'Now!' he said, 'YOU! Madam in the front.'

The old woman who was knitting in the second row looked up over her glasses.

'Yes, you. May I have your bag, please?'

The old woman looked around like someone who had been singled out by a teacher.

'May I have your bag?'

The old lady stuffed her knitting into her pocket and hauled herself to her feet. She picked up her bag and walked through the gaggle of children on the floor who parted like the red sea with her every step. They watched her as she handed her bag to Dad.

Dad took it and thanked her before waving his magic wand over the bag and reaching in. First, he took out a small flask of tea. The old lady blushed at that, but Abby couldn't blame her, the prices they charged for a cup of tea around here were extortionate.

Then came a half-eaten scone with jam, a pair of reading glasses, a puzzle book, a handkerchief, and

eventually . . . a fluffy pair of ears . . . as Dad pulled out . . . Ta-da, who looked positively disgruntled having spent the last five minutes in an old lady's handbag.

The old woman gasped and the crowd started to clap enthusiastically. There were even a few cheers!

'And now for the grand finale!' he announced. The audience were starting to eat out of Dad's hands by now, and Abby could see that he was feeding off the energy. When a show was going well, her dad would glow. It was like he transformed somehow into the Great Ronaldo. Not Dad, not the one who made her food or told her to do her homework, but a black-silk-cape-wearing, red-ribboned-top-hat-doffing magician.

Dad grinned at the audience as he placed Ta-da gently back in the box and replaced the lid. Then he swirled the magic wand around as if stirring some kind of mystical soup.

'This rabbit will take flight. It will become at one with the air!' he announced.

This was the hardest bit of the routine. Abby knew that. Dad knew that. All kinds of things could go wrong and had gone wrong in practice. Abby watched, suddenly tense again. A respectful hush had now fallen over the audience and even Little Mike looked like he was holding his breath.

'Go on little rabbit! FLY!' Dad shouted at last, flicking his wand upwards dramatically.

Suddenly, there was a green-and-red flash and a bang loud enough to blow your granny's socks off. Then came the smoke. Abby's heart beat painfully as she watched. The bang was supposed to happen, the flash too, but then the lid was supposed to come off the box. It was supposed to come off! But it looked as if it was jammed shut. It was then that the box started to move, jittering about on the table back and forth. Abby looked on as her dad started to panic. The little children at the front began to cough as rolling waves of smoke billowed their way off the stage towards them.

Dad tried again. 'Go little rabbit! FLY!' he shouted, waving his wand in the air.

Abby's heart sank. She could hardly see him now. The smoke cylinder had gone haywire and was spewing thick, choking smoke. There was some jeering from the crowd. The box was bouncing. Up and down and up and down as Dad fought to prise the lid off. Some of the littlest children were crying and the knitting lady was holding her handkerchief to her mouth.

'What's wrong with this thing?' She heard Dad's strangled voice say as he wrestled with the box.

Then, eventually, he managed to prise the lid off and, as he did, six pigeons burst from the box in a blind panic, feathers flying everywhere as they wheeled about in the smoke, disorientated. The boos were getting louder now, and Abby could see Dad trying to whistle to the pigeons to calm them down. Most magicians used doves, but since they were so expensive, Dad had plumped for pigeons and, because he'd bought them from an ex-racing-pigeon man, they weren't exactly cooperative. The bang had obviously given them the fright of their lives, and they were flying upwards, trying to get away as quickly as possible. The whole ordeal had obviously upset their tummies too, and Abby watched in horror as they splatted the audience below with their wet birdy poop.

'ARGHHH! NOOOO!' Shrieks arose from the audience as mums started gathering up their bags, and dads and uncles scooped up children left, right and centre, while the older children laughed hysterically.

Dad looked on in silent terror, as children and adults screamed. Little Mike was looking furious; he'd gone from a deep mahogany tan to a puce, and was pulling at his starched little collar. He was shouting at someone to put the lights on and waving his hands over his head.

It was then that Abby realized that some of the pigeons had singed their tail feathers. The spark that was supposed to ignite the small amount of gunpowder they used for the bang and light effect must have set them alight. Their feathers were actually smoking, and Abby watched in dismay as they flapped closer and closer to the smoke detectors on the ceiling.

What happened next seemed to play out in slow motion. Abby and Dad watched, hearts in mouths, as the sprinkler system switched on, sending water raining down on everyone beneath. Then, one sprinkler set off another and another until it looked like it was pouring with rain inside the entertainment hall. The fire alarms started blaring and Little Mike stood, mouth agape as the holidaymakers pushed past him, soggy and coughing and covered in bird poo, looking to all the world like they'd just survived the sinking of the Titanic.

Abby slipped through the curtains and caught Ta-da, who had reappeared and gone to hide under the table. She pulled him out and held him as he pushed his head under her armpit. Abby and Dad looked out at the empty hall, the rain still falling from the sky and where Little Mike stood, his suit soaking wet, looking like he was just about to explode.

CHAPTER TWO

It had taken them HOURS to clean up and to coax the pigeons back into their cage. Ta-da was now sleeping in Abby's lap in the front seat of the van and the pigeons were cooing resentfully in the back, still smelling a bit smoky. Abby looked up to see Dad making his way across the car park, his shoes still full of water, each squelchy step a reminder of what had just happened. He got in and closed the door without saying a word.

'I mean . . .' started Abby, 'I mean, it wasn't that bad . . . The first part was excellent. I thought you and Ta-da did brilliantly . . .'

Abby stroked Ta-da's ears thoughtfully.

'It was only the last bit that was a tad . . . under-whelming . . .'

She could almost hear Dad considering her words,

11

'Underwhelming? Underwhelming?!'

He rubbed his face with his palms, 'It was absolutely awful, Abby . . . I mean it couldn't really have gone any worse.'

He looked at her then, and Abby figured she may as well level with him, 'Actually you're right, Dad. It was awful. It was . . . diabolical . . . A shambles . . . An absolute disaster. To be honest, if there'd been a bucket of sand there, I'd have stuck my head into it like an ostrich and pretended I didn't exist.'

Dad grinned broadly at her and they held each other's gaze a moment. 'So, I'm guessing Little Mike doesn't want us back?' asked Abby, finally.

'I think we're actually pretty lucky he doesn't want to sue us . . . But no, we won't be coming back.'

Abby thought about this for a minute. How their income depended on getting a regular show. Children's birthday parties were all well and good, but it was difficult to make plans without regular money coming in.

'Don't look so worried,' said Dad gently, 'we'll work something out.'

Abby nodded.

'Right,' said Dad wearily, 'let's go home.'

Dad started the engine and Abby leant her head on the window and watched as the night flickered by. Although she could never imagine taking to the stage herself, she'd always loved going to work with Dad. Watching the sleight of hand he used to switch objects, the illusions and decoys. The way things worked, how a show was put together. She also loved hanging around in the green room watching dancers get ready. Looking at their costumes. Playing cards with the comedians and learning all of their really corny jokes. It was like all these people would come together as a kind of family. A night-time family. One that got together backstage at theatres and caravan parks and night clubs. When Abby was small, it felt like they were always surrounded by people, but now with all the flashy magic around on the telly and the street magic on the internet it felt like there were fewer and fewer live shows happening. It seemed like everyone was getting a bit jaded and, well, harder to impress.

Abby's favourite part had always been what they called in the business, the 'get-ins' and the 'get-outs'. The preparation the day before, planning the routine, and carrying all the equipment into the rusty old van. Then the drive, finding the venue, pulling all of the equipment out of the van and setting up the stage, and carrying the equipment back into the van at the end of the night and then the journey home. Just the two of them, talking about how well the night had gone, what they'd do differently next time. They'd learnt over the years to plan their stops, always somewhere they knew there'd be a chip shop open at midnight, and then they'd buy bottles of lemonade and drink them, Abby's feet up on the dashboard, both too full of adrenaline and applause and fizziness to be tired.

More recently though, Dad had become quieter. He'd have fewer new ideas and Abby knew that tonight had hurt. She could tell that he was getting kind of tired of the same old routines and the same faint applause. She could understand it too. The world which had seemed to her so glossy and shiny and sequinney when she was small just felt a little faded. A little threadbare. Tonight had felt like Dad's last real chance of making something of his magic; now it just felt like the end of something.

Abby listened to the van's engine struggling up a hill

as her dad changed gear. The pigeons had gone quiet now and Abby felt Ta-da's warmth in her lap.

'I never liked that Little Mike anyway . . .' she murmured.

'Thanks, Abby-cadabra . . .' Dad looked over and smiled.

'We'll be ok you know, I promise . . .' he said.

Abby smiled softly back.

'I know.'

CHAPTER THREE

Abby opened her eyes and stretched lazily. Judging by the light, she'd slept in a bit, and she could hear noises outside the bus. She hauled herself onto her elbow, pulled back the curtain and saw Dad carrying things out of the back of the van and into the rickety old shed he had built in order to store all his magical equipment. She listened as he walked back and forth from the van to the shed, talking to himself ten to the dozen as he usually did when he was trying to figure something out.

Abby and Dad lived on a bus. A real actual bus. Mum and Dad had bought it before Abby was born, partly because they couldn't afford to buy an actual house and partly because they were planning on saving up some money to spend a couple of years exploring the world together. And it must have been a very impressive bus when it was new. It was the square old-fashioned type, bright blue, with a red stripe running down the outside that kind of matched the old van.

In the back of the bus there was a bed on each side with a curtain in between for privacy and a shelf under the window for Abby's books. They'd lived there perfectly happy as a family and had almost saved up enough money for the big trip when Mum, well . . . she just died. Abby still couldn't believe it sometimes. One minute she was there and the next, poof! She was gone. Disappeared. Abby was still small and her dad had explained to her that something had happened in her brain. The only thing Abby really remembered about that time was asking Dad to magic her back, and Dad saying that it didn't work that way.

So the bus had stayed in the same place, the tyres had gone flat and they kind of got used to the idea of staying put. Dad had built a shed next to the bus to work on his magical equipment and soon it was time for Abby to start in the local school, and that was that.

*

Abby stretched out again before swinging her legs over the side of the bed and plopping to the floor. She walked to the front of the bus squeezing past Dad's still-soggy cape that he'd hung up to dry.

'Morning,' said Abby as she emerged from the bus and sat on the bottom step, squinting in the bright light. Dad didn't even look up; he was so preoccupied talking to himself he hadn't heard her. Abby watched as he pulled out a 'saw a person in half' box from the back of the van before disappearing back into the dusty old shed.

'Oh!' he said when he finally reappeared, 'there you are!' He smiled distractedly before moving towards the back of the van once more.

'What are you doing?' Abby asked.

The mumbling started again as he disappeared into the echoey van.

The van was slowly rusting and the massive magic wand painted on the side with the words, 'The Great Ronaldo' looked a bit flaky, but it still had a certain charm. They used it for carrying everything they needed to and from shows. It might be chains and a straitjacket for escape tricks, or it could be card tricks, or boxes for switching tricks. When Mum was around, there were more too; she specialized in using silver cups and balls for disappearing tricks and

there was also a wooden box which she made Dad sit in while she dramatically slid swords into it.

The business of magic was actually in Mum's blood. She was the one who had been brought up with it. Not that she was actually magic. Well, Abby didn't think so at least, although Dad always used to say that she was while looking at her soppily. Dad had learnt everything from her and they had, unusually for the time, become a partnership. A dynamic duo, as Dad liked to say. After all, Abby's mum would have never been happy being a 'pretty' assistant like so many other women in the magic world. No, they shared the stage together and Abby had so many vivid memories of watching her mum turn from, well, just Mum into Magic Mum. Wearing outfits that could be seen from the back of the audience. Sequins and mesh, feathers and fake fur, all

19

part of the spectacle. The shinier, the glossier, the better. Mum emerging from a straitjacket like a butterfly from a chrysalis while dangling upside down. Mum appearing as if from nowhere on a balcony when a few seconds earlier she'd been on the stage.

Out came Dad again.

'I'm almost finished,' he said distractedly as he carried some stocks into the shed.

By the time he finally emerged, the van was completely empty, and he looked exhausted. He smiled uncertainly as he walked towards her.

'I need to talk to you,' he said. In Abby's experience, these few words never led to anything great. No-one ever said, 'I need to talk to you, here's a thousand pounds', or, 'I need to talk to you, you never have to go to school again'.

'What have I done?' asked Abby, her stomach tightening a little.

'It's nothing you've done, quite the opposite actually.'

He'd started pacing now, which was making Abby even more nervous.

'Dad? What's wrong?' Abby watched him going

back and forth for a while.

'I . . . I'm going to get a job,' he said, his eyes finding hers.

Abby looked at him, a frown forming.

'But, you've got a job.'

He was pacing faster now.

'I mean,' said dad 'a proper job, in an office or a shop or something. I've got an appointment at the jobcentre tomorrow.'

He walked some more before coming to a dead stop in front of her.

'Well, say something then.'

Abby thought. Thought about what he might want her to say.

'What do you think?' he asked.

Abby shrugged. 'I don't know.' She was telling the truth. She kind of thought it might come to this one day, but now it had, it was a shock.

'The thing is—' he looked pained now – 'the thing is, I've been trying to keep the show on the road, been trying to keep things going but it's just not working out.' His eyes were darting everywhere.

'You're growing up, you'll need money for

school, trips, clubs, college.'

'It's just . . . Your mum and me, we started this when we were young—' he looked around as if searching for the words – 'maybe, maybe it's time I grew up too.'

He was holding out his hands in front of him now and for the first time in her life Abby thought that he looked a little older.

'Didn't Mum used to say that growing up was a trap?' asked Abby with a sad smile.

Dad laughed, then his gaze dropped to the floor.

'You're right, and she escaped it, didn't she?'

Abby's smile softened.

'I don't know, Abby. It's just, when your mum and I were doing shows, the audience was with us. They were there, on our side. There was this hush, this leaning in. They wanted to believe, wanted to be confounded.'

He wouldn't look at her now.

'I still feel it fleetingly some nights, but usually I feel like I may as well be in that room alone. You've felt it too, haven't you?'

Abby nodded reluctantly.

'I just wanted to say sorry.'

Abby looked at him, a question forming. 'For what?'

'For having to give up . . . For not being good enough . . .'

Abby felt the tears spring to her eyes.

'Dad, you don't have to be sorry.'

He shrugged. 'I just feel like I've let you down, that's all.'

Abby got up and ran barefoot towards him.

'There is no way you've let me down, ok?'

He held her for a moment before kissing her head.

'Are you sure?'

'Of course I am . . .' Abby said before giving him a hug.

They stood a moment, arms around each other, listening to the pigeons in the coop behind them cooing softly.

Dad spent the rest of the day staring at a blank piece of paper trying to make a list of what skills he had. He wanted to be prepared for his appointment at the jobcentre.

'It's no good,' he said scratching his head, 'I can't think

of anything I'm actually good at . . .'

Abby thought a minute.

'You're good at pulling rabbits out of a hat.'

Dad laughed. 'Well, I can't put that down, can I?'

'Oh, I don't know,' Abby frowned, 'I'd say that's dealing with the unexpected.'

Dad's eyes lit up, a slow smile spreading, 'Well, my goodness, you may be onto something there.' He licked the nib of the pencil and started scribbling.

Then, he looked up eagerly. 'How about sawing people in half?'

Abby thought hard.

'Resolving conflict.'

'Isn't it creating conflict?' quizzed Dad.

'Not when you put them back together!'

Dad laughed. 'Brilliant, utterly brilliant. How about escaping from chains?'

'Problem solving,' giggled Abby.

'Card tricks?'

'Good at mathematics.'

'Making things disappear?'

'Experience with removals.'

24

Together, they slowly filled up the paper, and by the end Dad had quite a roll call of impressive skills.

'Well,' he said, puffing out his chest a little, 'that should do it! If they don't give me job after all that then they're utterly bonkers.' And he wandered off to make them some tea.

Abby watched as the late evening light moved around the bus. Over the years since Mum had died, the bus had changed. Dad had built a tiny little shower, the footprint of which was not much bigger than a postage stamp, and placed a sofa and an old TV set with a twisted wire aerial that hung out of the window and made the old bus look like a caterpillar with one wonky antenna. More recently, Dad, being Dad, had made a series of tunnels all around the bus for Ta-da so he could hop about the place and not get lost.

Every wall was covered in posters of magic shows. Old ones from when the magicians were the biggest acts in town. Dog-eared and fading posters of famous magicians like Houdini in a clear box of water, upside down and in chains, his face contorted with a mixture of fear and theatricality. There were also images of the old fire kings and queens who could walk into massive ovens carrying steaks, stand there as if they were waiting for a bus and walk out again with the steak perfectly cooked on a plate. There were posters of sword swallowers, and a man called Dufour, who in his last appearance in Paris ate a plateful of iron nails garnished with glowing coals, which he crunched like you and I would crunch popcorn.

One of Abby's favourites though was of a lady named Thardo who let poisonous snakes bite her yet seemed completely unharmed, and even carried her lipstick in a snakeskin handbag. Her hair was perfectly coiffed and at her neck was a glowing emerald necklace with a snake eye at its centre. The posters were glowing now in the last light of day, the faces on them like people that Abby used to know.

Abby watched as Dad brought over their food, which they ate in a comfortable silence.

'It's for the best,' he said softly after a while.

'Of course it is,' replied Abby.

'You know what?' he said, reaching over and touching her hand, 'I really don't know what I'd do without you.'

*

That night Dad tucked her into bed like he still always did. And then, even though she was a little old for it now, he made her a balloon animal to sleep with. Abby smiled as he blew up the balloon before hiding it behind his back to start the twisting. Within moments, he presented her with a balloon tiger. Abby took it in her hands and looked at it.

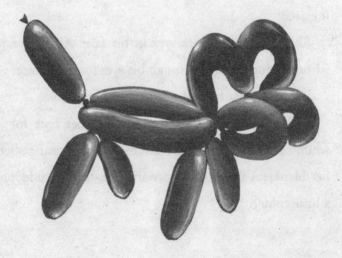

'Thanks, Dad.'

Abby watched him turn to switch off her lamp, a question forming on her lips that had been troubling her all day.

'Dad?'

He looked back at her in the half light.

'What is it my lovely?'

'Do you still think there's magic?'

Abby saw his blue eyes look suddenly worried. His face still.

'I mean not tricks and illusions like you and Mum . . . like we used to do . . . but real magic . . . Do you think it exists?'

Abby saw the uncertainty in his face. All the years without Mum flashed through his eyes for a moment.

'I don't know,' he said gently, 'but I hope so . . .'

He half-smiled at her and stroked her hair for a while before leaving. Abby lay in the dark and pulled her blanket a little tighter around her, feeling suddenly a little colder.

CHAPTER FOUR

Myra was waiting for Abby by the old bandstand. You couldn't really miss Myra because she always looked amazing. Her mum and dad ran a dry cleaners' on a side street off the promenade, and since they also did simple repairs, her mum, Deepa, had taught her how to sew. Myra was a keen learner, and by the time she was seven she was already using the sewing machine herself and making her own school bags. By eleven she had started customizing her own clothes. Abby's smile broadened when she saw her. Today, she was wearing a denim jacket covered in patches of colourful fabric and white trousers with a sequinned tuxedo stripe on each leg. Abby loved to see what she would wear in summer as the dull grey school uniforms they had to wear gave way to a whole six weeks' worth of possibilities.

'So, it was a disaster then?' Myra said, scrunching up her face.

'How do you know?'

'The videos are all over the internet. I even heard customers in the shop talking about it.'

Abby's shoulders fell, and she felt a heat coming to her chest and neck.

'Oh great,' she said. 'Fabulous. That's just brilliant.'

'Well, thank your lucky stars that all the kids have until September to forget,' Myra said, flashing her warmest smile. 'And don't worry, I still like you.'

'Even though me and Dad are complete losers?'

Myra beamed then, 'Especially because you're a pair of tragic losers.'

'Seriously though,' she asked, 'is your dad ok?'

Abby shrugged trying to think of the words while Myra waited for an answer.

'Abby?'

'Er, he's ok.'

Myra narrowed her eyes, 'Abby?'

'Umm, well he's actually thinking about giving up.'

Myra did a double take. 'What do you mean, giving up?'

She emphasized the last two words as if they tasted unpleasant. 'He can't! Magic isn't just what he does . . . It's who he is.'

Over the years, Myra had been to so many of Dad's shows. She loved everything about them, the loading and unloading the van, the tricks, the way the audience gasped and the long journeys home with Abby and her dad. Myra and Abby would both sit in the back of the van singing songs really really badly and really really loudly, while Dad pretended to be a DJ introducing the Terrible Top Ten. The magic shows had been part of both their lives for a long time.

Myra looked deep in thought.

'I just can't quite get my head around it,' she said, silently linking her arm in Abby's.

They walked along the promenade together, watching the first of the tourists carry their heaving bags to the beach, as if they were moving in for a fortnight rather than going for the day.

The town was like a grand old lady who used to have money. It still had a faded beauty and glamour but was now neglected and run down and had become somehow irrelevant. Even so, Abby loved the seafront, even in its dilapidated state. She liked to think it was an illusion itself – its dramatic frontages hiding the very ordinary lives of those living behind them. The promenade stretched like a stage, the set-dressing of the buildings behind, and the people all tiny in their colourful clothes strutting their stuff.

They passed the ancient pier. It looked like it had struck out confidently into the sea in a straight line before losing confidence, becoming thinner and more rickety and then fading into nothing. On it was a fruit machine place where you could play two-penny push and try and win a teddy bear, and a pavilion for performances, which was just about holding on. Outside were benches where old people sat in pairs eating chips and trying to shoo away the seagulls.

It was then that Abby saw them. She gave Myra a nudge and started walking faster but it was too late, they'd already been spotted.

'Hey Abby!' came a voice. Abby's blood ran cold. It was Jasmine, one of the mouthiest kids in her class. In a town this small, even the summer holidays couldn't completely rid you of the school bullies.

'You look a bit damp.'

There were only three of them: Jasmine, Ella and Josh, but it seemed like they took up all the space wherever they were. In school, they dominated the classroom and the canteen, and in town they seemed to roam the promenade like sharks looking for smaller fish to eat. Abby and Myra kept walking, trying not to look back as they started following them.

Abby felt Myra hold her arm a little tighter as if to say, 'Don't react. It's ok.'

'Can anyone smell bird poo?' The giggling came again, and this time Abby felt sick.

When she was younger, having a dad that was a magician was kind of cool. All the mums and dads in primary school would want him to do their kids' birthday parties, and Dad was more than willing to help. In return, they looked after Abby sometimes, taking her to school concerts or picking her up from places when Dad was busy. Now she was older though, having a magician for a dad was definitely not cool and some of the kids in school and around town really loved to remind her of it.

'How's the Rubbish Ronaldo?' It was Ella's voice this time. Josh, whom Abby had once considered to be ok, never said anything. But then he didn't try to stop Ella or Jasmine either.

'Is your dad still playing magician?' That was enough for Myra. She stopped, turned and squared up to the bullies.

'How about you lot go back to taking selfies and looking at yourselves, eh?'

Ella and Myra eyeballed each other for a second until Jasmine flicked her hair and pushed past them rolling her eyes.

'Nice outfit by the way,' Jasmine sniped as they moved away.

Abby watched them go, a trembling in the pit of her stomach, and nodded her thanks to Myra. Myra nodded back.

'Gosh they're so ANNOYING!' fumed Myra. 'Come on, I need ice-cream.'

Abby started to explain that she didn't have any money but Myra interrupted her.

'It's ok, Mum gave me some change from the tip jar, for both of us. Let's go . . .'

Abby watched her go and, in that moment, she thanked her lucky stars for a friend like Myra.

CHAPTER FIVE

A bby called for Dad but he was nowhere to be seen. She gave Ta-da the core of the apple she'd been eating on the walk home before tickling his ear and walking to the shed. The shed roof was zinc iron, which rat-tat-tatted when it rained, and there was a wonky wooden door that you had to drag shut because it didn't hang properly. The pigeon loft was tucked behind the front door on the left so that when Dad let them out, they could fly through the rickety door and into the sky. On the other side of that was an old temperamental washing machine that Dad would bow to and thank after he unloaded it, hoping that good manners might keep it going a few years longer. Dad had cobbled the shed together from bits of timber and sheets of plywood that he had found over the years, and he kept adding to it until it was around the length of the bus and twice as wide. It was shabby and haphazard, but it was part of their home. The overspill of their lives on the bus. Their memories and their history.

There were shelves and shelves of things that Dad had collected over the years as well as things that they had inherited from Mum's side of the family. There were boxes and old suitcases and chests full to the brim with costumes and props and tricks and cards and goodness-knows-what. Abby leant on the doorframe. The shed was in an even greater mess than usual!

'What on earth are you doing?' she asked.

Dad was on his knees, an open suitcase in front of him. He was scratching his head.

'I'm sure I had a suit here somewhere. The one I wore when I married Mum. I wonder where she put it?'

Abby watched as he rifled through the suitcase.

'I'm going to need one for tomorrow, I've got an interview.'

'So I take it the jobcentre went well?'

Dad smiled.

'Where's the interview?'

'The care home down by the pier.'

'The care home?'

Dad shrugged. 'Might be good, and there's not much work around.'

'Why do you want your wedding suit?' asked Abby.

Dad smiled, 'Well, Abby-cadabra, all my other suits are either covered in sequins, glitter or are bright-pink-and-purple.'

Abby smiled. 'Oh, I see your point.'

'I've been looking all day, and I just can't seem to find it.' Abby could see that he was tired.

'Do you want me to look?' she asked.

'You know what? I could do with a cup of tea,' he gasped. 'My mouth's as dry as a camel's armpit.'

Abby smiled as she watched Dad head for the bus, before walking into the cool dusty darkness of the shed, her eyes adjusting slowly.

She had spent hours in here. Hours and hours playing and pretending and reading. There was supposed to be a little clearing in the middle but because finding things had never been Dad's strong suit, there were now open suitcases and cardboard boxes all over the floor.

Abby set about closing some of them so she could start searching a little more methodically, and that's when Abby unearthed her favourite old trunk. She smiled as she took in the stickers on it. An elegant lady on a bike in front of the Eiffel Tower, a handsome blonde skier in the Alps, and wonderful images of the Great Wall of China under looming skies. It had belonged to Abby's grandmother. She had been a traveller, a performer, a dancer and a puppeteer. She had brought up Abby's mum in the middle of it all and Mum had cherished her things. Abby hauled it towards her and, although she had looked through it a thousand times, she still felt an excitement in her tummy every time she opened it. She knew it was unlikely Dad's suit would be in it, but she couldn't resist.

Abby pulled out some red silk dresses trimmed with black fringe and some old scores from musicals with curly Victorian writing and pictures of forget-me-nots on the front. Then there were letters. Letters from Abby's grandmother to her mum. Crayoned pictures from Abby's mum's childhood. There were boxes of buttons and silk scarves and puppets with their faces thickly painted, their smiles frozen in time, their strings all tangled. There were books with flowers pressed paper-thin between the pages and scarves of intensely coloured silk. Abby's favourites, though, were the pairs of dancing shoes, their soles worn cloudy from dancing on stages long ago in faraway places. Abby smiled at them. Felt for a moment the warmth of those concert halls and theatres. She could almost hear the applause. Then Abby remembered the suit. She closed the trunk and clicked it shut.

Looking around once again, she pulled another box towards her, losing herself in the task at hand. Eventually, her knees started aching and she realized it was getting dark. She'd completely lost track of time. She got up,

brushing the dust from the knees of her trousers. She moved towards the doorway and was about to switch off the light when she heard a noise behind her. She turned, thinking it must be the pigeons, but they were roosting quietly in their loft. She looked back to see her grandmother's trunk. The lid was open. Abby looked again. She was sure she had closed it. It was domed and heavy – it didn't open easily. She frowned before walking back towards it.

She looked in. There was nothing but the clothes and the puppets and the letters. She closed it again, pushing her weight down on it this time, making sure the old brass catch clunked satisfyingly. Happy, she walked back towards the doorway only to hear the sound again. This time she froze. Her skin tingling. Slowly, she turned, and to her astonishment, the lid was open again. Her heart started pounding and she stood frozen for a moment, her stomach tightening. She felt something stir inside her. It wasn't fear. It was compulsion. A need to know. The trunk was drawing her towards it. She inched closer, slowly, slowly, and peered into the trunk, and there on top of the red silk dresses was a small box she had never seen before.

Abby blinked, stared through the half-light, a cold sweat forming on her back. She felt her hand reach out, the tips of her fingers getting closer and closer, and then she flicked off the lid. Inside was a book. Abby gasped. It was definitely there, and it had most definitely not been there two minutes before. It was a deep brown with strange

signs carved into the leather cover. Abby reached out her hand and touched it. She felt deep down that somehow it belonged to her. She took it in her hands. There were no words on the cover, just a moon and stars and the carved markings. She opened it, and on the stiff paper pages, there were rows and rows of letters, or symbols, writing in a language she didn't understand.

'No sign of it then?'

Abby almost jumped out her skin. It was Dad. She pushed the book into the back waistband of her trousers.

'You've been in here absolutely ages,' he said, squinting into the gloom. As her face came into focus, he noticed how pale she was.

'Blimey! You ok? You look like you've seen a ghost!'

'I'm fine!' she squealed, as her voice had gone all funny.

'If you say so,' he answered, looking at her quizzically.

'Did you find it?' he asked again.

'Find what?'

'The suit. My suit?'

'Oh, no!' She'd forgotten all about it.

'Well, come on then,' Dad said, looking at her, bewildered, 'it's time for bed.'

43

Abby nodded.

'I'll be there now.'

Dad turned to go, and when she was sure he was gone, she reached behind her and pulled the book from her waistband. It felt heavy and solid in her fingers, the gold symbols glittering on the cover in the last light of day.

CHAPTER SIX

Afternoons had always been Myra's favourite time in the shop, and she never passed up the opportunity to help out, because once the morning and lunchtime rushes had passed, with Myra and her parents frantically trying to match the right clothes to the right people, the shop would take on a different personality, in Myra's mind anyway. It was when the designer in her was filled with inspiration, when she'd have time to take in the fabrics, feel their textures, to study the cut and stitching of every piece. She liked nothing better than to take an old dress or top and sit quietly with it in her lap for a moment, and just kind of 'listen' to it. She would try and understand the life it had had and what it had the potential to be. In those quiet moments, the fabric would almost start to speak to her. Ideas would begin to fizz up inside her about how she could cut and customize it, how she could change and transform it.

Of course, not all the clothes whispered to her. There was always the boring stuff – the work shirts, the pinstripe suits and the winter coats, but Myra would look past those, her eyes drawn to the wedding dresses waiting to be dry-cleaned and folded in tissue paper so that they could be treasured by daughters and daughters' daughters. Then there would be ballgowns, sequinned and silky, designed with full skirts so they would flow on the dancefloor and become almost extensions of the dancers who wore them. Myra loved the clothes from different cultures too. Sometimes, they'd get wax-printed African fabrics full of joyous colours and flowers and leaves, and head-wraps that were so long Myra would always wonder how their owners could tie them so neatly. Then there were the saris, long lengths of jewel-coloured silk encrusted with gold and silver decorations. Her mother was the specialist with those, maintaining the beadwork and disguising any stains on the silk. Clothes weren't just clothes. They meant something. Myra could feel it. They told the world who you were and how you were feeling.

But the best thing about working in the shop was that every garment they cleaned or repaired had to be collected within four months, or it would be given to charity or thrown away. The shop was small and storage was limited, so her mum and dad would assume that after four months whatever it was it must be unwanted. Myra had persuaded her parents to let her have first pick of anything that was going to be sent to the charity shop, and then she'd lovingly, delicately, expertly take the garments apart before using the fabric in her own designs.

It was quiet this afternoon, and Myra had gently encouraged her parents to go upstairs so she could have some peace and quiet to get some work done. She pulled out her sketchbook and placed it on the counter, then unravelled a long garment which was the beginnings of a dress. In the past months, she had found herself becoming more and more confident in customizing clothes for herself, and with that success came a new feeling of restlessness. She'd been having thoughts about designing her first actual collection of clothes just like Masaba Gupta or Vivienne Westwood. A collection of clothes designed by her from scratch. But although she was happy with the sketches she had made, and the rough patterns she had on brown paper, she just didn't seem to be able to construct what she had imagined in her head.

When designers made new clothes, they made them up first out of cheap white cotton so they could make sure the design worked before using more luxurious fabrics, and although Myra had stayed up way past her bedtime last night trying to sort it out, the dress was still an awful jumbled mess. It seemed that customizing clothes for herself was one thing, but designing for other people? Well, it was waaaaay more complicated than she had imagined.

'Myra?' She hadn't heard her mum's footsteps on the stairs behind her. 'It's time for food.'

Myra looked up and nodded.

'What have you got there?' asked her mum as she walked across the shop to lock the door and turn over the OPEN sign.

Myra pulled the dress into her lap to hide it. 'Oh, nothing,' she said as the door clunked shut. Her mum smiled at her.

'Ok, well, you show me when you're ready . . . Thanks for helping with the shop today,' Mum said, 'it gave your father and me some time to sort things out upstairs.'

'Is everything ok?' Myra asked. Even though she'd been preoccupied with her work, she had noticed that her mum and dad had been having some hushed conversations lately.

Her mum smiled tiredly. 'Of course. Now come on, let's go upstairs. I'm starving.'

Abby hadn't slept much. She'd shoved the book down between her mattress and the wall of the bus, and all night she'd been reaching down just to check if (a) it was still there and (b) it was actually real. She'd lain, listening to Dad toss and turn ahead of his interview, trying to rationalize what had just happened. How the book had appeared as if from thin air. Then she'd eaten her cereal and watched as Dad prepared himself for his interview. He had found his suit eventually – it had been under his bed in a box all along – but he'd ignored the fact that he hadn't worn it since he was a young man, and he was a slightly different shape after all these years. He just about managed to get into it, but fashion had changed since then, so his collar was a little too wide and his tie was a little too narrow and shiny, making him look like he'd tied an eel around his neck. She told him that he looked fabulous, of course, and he bowed theatrically before righting himself in case he split the back of his trousers.

Abby had gone to look at the book a million times that morning, before going for a walk in the field around the bus to clear her head. As she wandered, she told herself the book had probably been there all along, that she just hadn't noticed it before, that it was just a regular book from Grandma's travels. It was from a faraway place and in a foreign language, that was all. Except something was bothering her. She liked languages. In fact, Abby was so interested in languages that her teacher, Mrs Mainwaring, had ordered in some specialist books for her. There was one on how different countries around the world wrote things down. Everyone had heard of Egyptian hieroglyphics and Chinese characters of course, but there were others too, more unusual ones. She'd seen pictures of the Cherokee language, which had curved letters like winding winds, and Lanna, a script from

Thailand, which was beautiful and rounded. But the symbols in this book? They didn't look like any of the alphabets she'd ever seen before. There were all sorts of other languages too, secret ones. Codes like Polari and Cockney Rhyming Slang. There were the silly made-up words her mum had used for things, and the shorthand that came so easily to the cool kids at school.

She sat down on the grass and watched the town down below a moment, trying to force her brain into rationalizing things, but it was no good. She had to have another look. She got up and jogged back to the bus, sprang up the steps, and quickly closed all the curtains, before scooping up Ta-da, who looked slightly startled at her sudden reappearance. She headed to the back of the bus, placed Ta-da on the bed and clicked on the lamp above her. Sitting cross-legged, she slid her hand down the side of the bed and pulled out the book to look at it again. It was so beautiful. She traced the golden letters and symbols with her fingertips before opening it up.

The paper inside was a creamy parchment, thick and substantial. And there were what seemed like three sections to it: one third of the pages were edged in gold, one third edged in silver and one third in copper. The end papers inside the cover were inky-blue like the night sky and studded with constellations of stars. It was stunning. Magical. Abby took it in for a moment, and turned to the title page and there were the symbols. The letters. All in neat rows. Some of the characters were curvy, some straight. Some were repeated, she could see that. She ran her fingers down the lines, thinking, thinking. The ink was a rich indigo colour. There were no smudges, no mistakes, although Abby was sure that it was handwritten with a fountain pen or a quill or something. She studied it closely under the spotlight of her lamp, vaguely aware of Ta-da moving about at the bottom of the bed. Then, suddenly, she felt dizzy.

Something was wrong.

She saw the letters moving. Changing.

Abby's stomach lurched and she instinctively looked away. She made herself count to ten. Then she turned her eyes back to the page . . . and sure enough, the words had rearranged themselves, now clumping together in sentences . . . They were looking much more like words that Abby could read now, but still in another language. She watched as they seemed to pulse, to form and reform in different configurations, until she was sure she recognized a French word . . . Then . . . a Spanish one? An English one?

And suddenly they became understandable, one line appearing after another:

See the magic on these pages
Three spells cherished through the ages.
Practise them well, but use with care,
Once performed they disappear

Abby was breathing fast and shallow, and she could feel a tingling along every inch of her skin . . .

Three spells?

'Guess what?' She hadn't even heard Dad come into the bus. She spun around, her heart still in her mouth, to see him standing, his tie pulled loose and two packets of sweaty fish and chips in his hands.

'Guess who got the job? Come on! Celebratory fish supper it is! I could only afford one fish so we're going to have to share it, but if you ask me it tastes better that way anyway.'

'You ok?' he asked as he started rattling in the drawer for forks.

'Yup,' said Abby, her voice a little strangled, 'absolutely.'

'Well come on then, tuck in.'

Abby stood as her dad started rustling the chip paper and looked back through the fading light at the book lying innocently on the bed.

CHAPTER SEVEN

Abby got up early and sat at the table, the book in front of her, watching as the darkness thinned around the bus. When she first awoke, the memories of last night were hazy, mixed up with the fish-and-chips steam on the windows and Dad's excitement at getting a new job. But she kept replaying the scene in her head when the ink moved and moulded into new words. In that moment it was almost like her feelings had overtaken her senses, and even this morning she could almost feel the tingling on her skin once again. Last night the book had become vital, alive, full of this indescribable electric energy. The ink had glowed, become fluid, the symbols liquid, but now, as dawn grew around the bus, the book looked . . . well . . . absolutely normal. She studied it in the grey light before reaching out her hand towards it, and tentatively touching it, much like you'd poke a spent firework, scared it might still go off. Nothing.

Dad started stirring and getting up. Abby slipped the book off the table and pushed it behind her back so that he wouldn't see it.

'Morning.' Dad was dressed in his new light-blue uniform of tunic and trousers which he'd lovingly ironed pleats into the night before. He filled the kettle and yawned, rubbing his belly before looking back at Abby.

'You're quiet,' he said.

'Am I?' she answered. Abby watched as he started to make them both tea and tried to put a packed lunch together from what meagre offerings the fridge had, without looking too weird on his first day. He had managed to gather a lump of cheese, a boiled egg, half a scotch egg and a yoghurt so far past its sell-by date it could probably have found its own way to work.

'You didn't eat much last night either,' said Dad. 'You ok?'

'I think so,' answered Abby truthfully.

He dried his hands on a tea towel and looked at her. 'You're very pale. I can stay home today if you want.

It's only an induction day. I could look after you.'

Abby shook her head.

'No, it's important that you go, learn the ropes. And anyway, I'm meeting Myra later.'

She tried to smile reassuringly. 'You'd better go or you'll be late.'

'Oh my god, is that the time? Ok,' he said, looking at his watch and leaning over to tip the rest of his tea down the sink. 'Ok, well, call me if you need me.'

Abby nodded.

'And wish me luck . . .'

Abby shook her head. 'Nope,' she said, 'because you won't need it.'

He came back to drop a kiss on her head and placed the palm of his hand on her forehead momentarily to check for a fever. 'You're alright,' he muttered, and then, 'Love you,' as he ran out the door.

'Love you too,' Abby said, her voice fading away.

Abby sat for a while after her father left, listening to the silence. Last night she had felt nothing but disbelief, then excitement, but this morning, she had an uneasy feeling deep down that she just couldn't shift. She tried to distract herself with cleaning out Ta-da's run, and was thankful when it was time to meet Myra. She walk-ran the whole way along the terrace behind the field and down into the town below, crossing the deserted streets on her way to the seafront.

The promenade was always empty first thing in the morning, with no sounds except for the sea's breathing and the scrape of cafe owners dragging their signs onto the pavement. There was the occasional dog walker and jogger, but apart from that it was totally still. Abby walked along the seafront for a moment before heading down some worn concrete steps to the beach where she scrunch-scrunched across the dark gravelly sand towards the pier. The pier was well past its prime, but here, underneath it, among the rusty girders covered in limpets and barnacles, Abby had always found a kind of haven. Even though it was always damp and soggy, it was out of sight, and safe from any marauding bullies. Abby also kind of liked the fact that you would hear people's footsteps on the pier boards above and catch snippets of their conversations while they had no idea she was there.

She pulled off her coat and laid it down before sitting on it. She looked out to sea. It seemed restless today, and because it was still early, it looked a little grey and muddy.

Seeing the promenade again, old memories of her mother began to swirl, much like the starlings that overwintered under the pier. First one, then two, then a dozen, until they were flying in formation. She thought about the way her stomach had leapt last night. The tingling on her skin. The dizzy feeling that made things feel unreal, and the problem was that deep down she knew she had felt that way before. That feeling of your senses doing something that you didn't quite understand . . .

Abby smiled softly as Myra approached and flopped down next to her. Myra sensed Abby's stillness, so they sat for a long while before Myra drew a deep breath.

'So, are we going to sit here in silence like a couple of weirdos or do you want me to go first?'

Abby smiled, 'You go,' she said.

Myra pulled her legs in towards her and crossed them.

'It's these designs I've been working on. They're so frustrating.'

Abby listened.

'It's like I can see everything in my head, but when I try and make them real everything falls apart. It's like I haven't got the skills to make what I'm imagining. Urgh!' she exclaimed.

'What about your mum? Can she help?' asked Abby.

Myra shrugged. 'She's a bit preoccupied with something at the moment . . . I mean, of course she'd help me, but it feels like something I need to figure out myself. If I'm going to be a designer one day.'

Abby nodded, looking back out to sea. 'I don't know how to tell you this, Myra. I don't know if you know . . .'

Myra turned her head and looked at her in concern.

'. . . but you're only twelve.'

Abby watched as Myra's face broke into a soft smile.

'I mean, I think you have time to learn all this stuff. People expect twelve-year-olds to be able to make beans on toast, and make their own beds and stuff, not to be able to make tuxedos from scratch.'

Myra laughed now, shrugged the tension from her shoulders and watched as Abby raked up a handful of sand and let it slip through her fingers.

They watched the sea a moment.

'So, what's bugging you?' Myra asked.

Abby's smile straightened. She thought for a moment, looked for the words as she watched a few seagulls being tossed around above the sea.

'I don't know . . . I'm just feeling a bit . . . weird,' she shrugged. 'Maybe it's all the change . . .'

Myra raised an eyebrow.

'About your dad giving up magic, you mean?'

'Yes . . . And . . .' She really wanted to tell Myra about the book, it was just that it sounded so silly. 'Well . . .' Abby looked out at the horizon, held it in her gaze to help her get the words out. 'When Mum died, I went through a period of seeing her in places. I don't know, I thought I saw her coattails among the crowd on the prom.'

Abby could feel Myra's eyes on her.

'Or, and this was really weird, sometimes I'd hear a laugh just like hers behind me and my heart would beat so fast, and I'd be convinced it was her. Or I'd accidentally put my hand up for her to hold when I was crossing a road.'

Abby could feel Myra's warmth beside her.

'It was my mind playing tricks on me because I wanted to see her so badly, but it hurt so much. After a while it stopped, but I just— I felt that way again last night about something, that's all. You start seeing things, hearing things. It's really weird.'

Myra nodded, squeezed Abby closer.

Abby shrugged. 'Sometimes, you want things so badly, your mind makes things up. You see signs that aren't there and it doesn't help you, it just makes things worse . . .'

Abby noticed that there were tears in Myra's eyes now. They sat in silence a moment.

'Well, on the upside, I feel better about my life now,' Myra said.

Abby laughed and leant her head on Myra, and they watched as the mist began to lift and the promenade became busier and sunnier.

'Like you said, maybe it's just all the change,' suggested Myra.

'Maybe,' whispered Abby.

They spent the rest of the day laughing on the swings in the empty kids' playground and drinking slushies that made their tongues blue, and afterwards, as she made her way home, Abby realized she felt much better. Spending time with Myra had that effect on her.

As she approached the bus, Abby saw Dad about to let the pigeons out for their evening flight. He smiled at her.

'Oh good, you've got more colour in your cheeks.'

Abby smiled back at him and walked to stand beside him. 'Yes, I'm feeling better, I think.'

The pigeons were rustling in their loft impatiently. They were very ordinary-looking in many ways. Their dull grey feathering, their dark eyes. It was only when they were set free that they shone. Their wings would burst open, and their iridescent collars would glimmer in jewel tones in the sun. It was like they were totally unremarkable until they were in their element and then they were extraordinary. They were scrabbling at the mesh window, their wings aching for flight, like there was something inside them that was inevitable somehow.

Then, Dad let them free and they exhaled into the sky. Dad's face was shining. He was whistling to himself, and Abby realized that she hadn't heard him do that for a very long time. Abby watched as he did a little dance and started to clean out the loft, his confidence starting to return. He smiled at her.

'It went well, then?' Abby asked.

'It was brilliant!' said Dad. 'Come and have a cuppa, I'll tell you all about it.'

Abby followed him onto the bus where he proceeded to make them a mug of tea each. Abby listened as he explained that he'd had to learn so many new things. How to help someone elderly to walk, how to help someone into and out of the bath.

'Jamal was an engineer and he's got these really cool ship plans on his wall; and then there's Beryl, she's such a lovely woman, she used to be a dancer; and Glenys, who's a bit of a character, she's started to call me her new toy boy . . .'

Abby listened. He was animated. Happy.

'There's a real sense of community there, you know?'

Abby nodded.

'And tomorrow, they might even let me do the tea trolley!'

Abby raised her eyebrows.

'Go Dad!'

Dad laughed.

'I don't know,' he said, looking thoughtful, 'I think that this is going to work out for us. It's hard to let go, but sometimes it's the only thing you can do.'

Abby looked at him, thoughts of the book swirling.

'You ok Abby-cadabra?'

It was stupid, she'd been deluding herself. The book was just a book.

'Yeah, I'm fine . . .'

Dad tilted his head and studied her before taking a slurp of tea.

'I was thinking too, about maybe selling a few bits of our magic stuff.'

Abby's heart jumped at this.

'It's just that we need the money, and being a carer isn't going to make us rich any time soon.'

'But . . . isn't it a bit soon to be thinking about selling?'

Abby watched as Dad shrugged. 'We've made the decision, haven't we?'

Abby thought a moment.

'Right,' he said, 'I need a shower so don't turn any of the taps on or you'll freeze me to death.'

Abby nodded and watched him go. She sat for a moment, looking at his empty mug. Thinking. Thinking. And when her dad slipped into the tiny postage-stamp-sized cubicle that was their shower, she walked towards her bed and pulled out the book. She looked at it and realized he was right. It was hard to let go, but they had to do it. She marched outside as the light was fading and walked into the shed. There, she hauled open Grandma's trunk and pushed the book right down into the bottom, out of sight and out of mind. Then she closed the lid and sat on it. Looking back out into the twilight, she saw the pigeons coming home to roost.

CHAPTER EIGHT

Myra wasn't expecting a full house when she got home. She heard the hum of discussion when she closed the door of the shop downstairs, crossed the floor and made her way up the stairs. She opened the flat door to be confronted with almost all of the adults in her extended family. There was a sudden hush as she walked in, followed by a flurry of exclamations of 'How are you?' and hugs and 'It's time you stopped growing'. Myra started to feel very uneasy. Everyone was in and out of each other's houses all of the time, and there was usually laughing, eating, arguing, watching TV and running around gardens with her cousins. This was different. Adults sitting around the table was serious business. It must've been extra serious business, because there wasn't even any food, and quite frankly, there was always food.

Myra sensed that she should probably make herself scarce and went to her bedroom. Afterwards, there was the tell-tale scraping of chairs on the floor, which signalled the discussion was over, so she opened the door a tiny amount and snuck her head in the gap to see her aunts and uncles embracing her mum and dad.

Myra stood in the doorway and listened as the footsteps receded on the steps, and then she found her dad's eyes on hers. He motioned for her to come out and, much to Myra's concern, her mum and dad sat down again. She did the same, her eyes scanning back and forth between their faces.

'Don't look so worried!' said Mum smiling. 'Your father and I just need to talk to you about something.'

Her father plaited his fingers on the table in front of him. Mum nodded at him and then nodded towards Myra.

'Well, go on then, tell her.'

Her father cleared his throat.

'Your mother and I have been thinking . . .'

Myra had never seen them so serious. She felt weak, a growing sense of dread. Her father swallowed hard . . .

'We've been thinking about buying a couple of donkeys.'

Myra frowned.

'Donkeys?' she exclaimed.

'Yes, donkeys. There's good money to be made from donkey rides on the prom. We could keep them in the shop downstairs.'

Myra couldn't believe her ears, she stared back at her father in complete silence . . .

'How do you feel about looking after them?'

'B-but . . .' stammered Myra, 'I don't know anything about donkeys!'

It was then that her dad's deadpan face burst into hysterical laughter.

'Sanjeev,' her mum said, poking him in the ribs, 'that isn't funny. Look at the girl.'

Her father was still laughing.

Myra sat back and crossed her arms, rolling her eyes.

'What is wrong with you?' she asked her dad, who was gasping for air by now.

'I don't know what's wrong with him,' answered Mum. 'I ask myself the same question several times a day.'

'I'm sorry, it was just that you looked so serious!' her dad said eventually. 'I couldn't resist.'

Then suddenly, Dad composed himself completely.

'Ok, I'm serious now, I promise.'

Myra nodded.

'Right, you know your cousin isn't well, don't you?'

Myra nodded. Her cousin Ishan was much older than her and had been unwell for a lot of his life.

'Well, he's been doing better recently, and there's a new medical trial out in America that his doctors think could make a massive difference.'

Myra nodded. 'That's really great.'

'Although I doubt if this treatment will cure his terrible taste in sci-fi films,' added her dad.

Myra smiled.

'The thing is,' continued Dad, 'the treatment is expensive. Really expensive. That's what the meeting was about today . . . We're all trying to work out how to help.'

'Okaaay,' answered Myra, wondering what this had to do with her.

'The reason we wanted to talk to you about it was that we've got some savings we'd been keeping for your education . . . and if we want to help Ishan, we'd have to use that pot and then some. That is to say, if we go ahead, things will get really tight around here. Really tight,' he emphasized. 'We just wanted to see how you felt about it before committing.'

'Give the money to Ishan,' Myra said immediately.

Dad looked at her mum and Myra saw tears spring to her mum's eyes.

'We wanted to talk to you, to involve you, you're growing up and decisions have to be made,' he said.

'Please, there's no decision to make,' said Myra. 'Things will work out, don't worry.'

It was her mother's turn to speak now.

'We aren't doing this lightly, you know that . . . your future is so important to us and I know you've had your heart set on doing fashion or textiles, and we'll find a way to make that happen, I'm sure.'

'Seriously, Mum,' Myra interjected. 'You know, I'm only twelve, things change . . . and college or uni is ages away. And anyway, who says I'd even be good enough to go?'

Deepa studied her more seriously now, 'We just don't

want you to give up any of your dreams over this Myra.'

'Mum, I know,' said Myra feeling a strange tightness in her throat.

'Ok then, well that's settled,' said Sanjeev. 'We really are very proud of you, you know.'

Myra smiled at them both, relieved that she finally knew what was going on.

'Right,' said Dad, slapping his knees with the palms of his hands, 'I'm making dinner tonight so get out of my kitchen.'

Mum did a silly gagging sign towards Myra and Dad went to put on his apron.

'And speaking of dinner,' he said, 'I need some tomatoes.' He put some money on the table for Myra who rolled her eyes and pocketed it.

'Get some chocolate for after food too. If you make it a big bar I might share it.' He winked at her.

Myra nodded. She walked down the stairs and heard her mum tying the apron around his waist and pulling it tight to make him fake scream in pain. She smiled and realized for a moment how much she loved them.

Myra walked down the stairs, unlocked the shop

72

door and crossed the road onto the promenade. She breathed in the salty air and felt her shoulders drop. At least she knew what had been going on. And she was so, so pleased for Ishan. Like her mum had said, things would be tight, but things had always been a little tight. They didn't really take holidays and the only luxury that her mum and dad had was the old motorbike and sidecar that Dad had kept from his youth. Dad would keep saying that it took up too much room, and that he should sell it, but Mum would always remind him soppily that it was the bike they had ridden on their first date. Myra smiled just thinking about them, and was nearly at the corner shop when she heard some voices behind her.

'Here she is,' sneered Jasmine. Myra turned. They were standing there chewing gum, looking delighted to have found Myra alone. The three of them walked closer.

'Look at you,' said Ella as Jasmine laughed.

'Always been a bit of a weirdo, haven't you? You and your home-made clothes.'

Jasmine laughed and moved closer. Myra really didn't need this today.

73

'Seriously? Can't your parents afford to buy you clothes from normal shops, or what?' Jasmine said again. Josh was behind them saying nothing.

'Just go away Jasmine,' Myra replied, feeling a flash of anger across her chest.

Jasmine laughed. 'Why? You going to make me?'

'I'm not scared of you,' Myra said, composing herself, and standing square now.

Jasmine hadn't bet on Myra answering back. Her smile straightened, then suddenly she pushed Myra, hard and spitefully. Myra fell backwards against an old bench on the prom. It tripped her, and she scraped her cheek against it as she fell.

Jasmine looked down at her. She'd pushed her denim jacket off her shoulder and her high ponytail was at an angle. Ella looked unsure behind her.

'Look at the state of you,' she spat, and with that, Ella and Jasmine turned and left. Josh stood for a moment, seemingly frozen to the spot. He looked at Myra as if about to speak, but he was summoned by Jasmine and trotted away obediently. Myra controlled her breathing and got to her feet. It wasn't just anger she was feeling, or even humiliation. She was so full of feelings she couldn't even untangle them all. She kicked the bench before leaning on it, breathing heavily and listening to the sea below.

CHAPTER NINE

Friday night had come around and Abby had made her way over to Aunt Linda's house for tea. Linda wasn't Abby's real aunt but she was Mum's oldest friend, the one who'd cooked for her when Mum died and stayed over for weeks afterwards. The one who had taught Dad how to plait Abby's auburn hair and had her for a sleepover once a week when she was younger so that Dad could have a rest. The kind of person who seemed to be able to say anything and everything because she had always been there, knew everything and you'd never be rid of her. Abby hadn't actually said she'd be over for food today but she knew it didn't matter – she knew Linda's door was always open.

'It's me!' shouted Abby.

'Tea's on,' came the reply.

Abby pulled off her shoes and threw her bag down at the bottom of the stairs. It was a terraced house with a narrow corridor, some spindly stairs and a small living room to the right. Abby had never really thought about it as small until she and Lenny, Linda's son, started to grow. She walked into the little living room and stepped over Lenny's legs as he lounged on the sofa like a piece of stretched gum, not lifting his eyes from his phone. Lenny had once been that annoying older brother figure, antagonistic with a talent for being spectacularly irritating. But recently he'd undergone a kind of transformation. It was as if his body had said, right, that's it, I'm off, and shot upwards, leaving his feet behind. His voice had deepened too, so he looked and sounded like a completely different person. Abby walked through to the narrow kitchen in the back and watched as Linda cooked.

'Lay the table will you?' she asked.

Abby rummaged in the cutlery drawer and watched as Linda added some extra potatoes to the corned beef hash she was making to bulk it out a little.

Linda was a local girl. She'd gone to school here and stuck around after Lenny was born when she was pretty young. She worked as a cleaner and was constantly skint, but she was an expert at stretching meals so far Abby was surprised they didn't snap. The thing about Linda, though, was that however little she had of anything, she always made it enough.

'So, has that father of yours come to his senses yet?' Linda asked curtly.

Abby tried to feign innocence.

Linda gave her a look. 'He phoned to tell me he'd given up. I've never heard such nonsense.'

When Aunt Linda was in a grump you had to treat her really really carefully so as not to detonate her like a bomb. Perhaps it was something to do with her tattoos or her bleach blonde hair, but Linda seemed like someone you wouldn't want to get on the wrong side of. She was protective and passionate, fierce but loyal. She'd take no nonsense but wouldn't hold a grudge either. She was both scary and soft, and Abby loved her for it.

'I told him he's doing the wrong thing . . . I spent an hour on the phone to the pillock . . .'

'You didn't actually call him a pillock, did you?'

'I might have.'

Abby rolled her eyes as she placed the knives and forks on the pull-down table.

'I haven't heard anything so ridiculous in my life. He's worked so hard at magic and to give it all up because of a bad show.'

'It wasn't just a bad show, Linda, it was a disaster.'

'I don't care, one bad show does not maketh the magician . . . or something like that—' she looked like she'd just confused herself a little – 'and he's not getting any younger either.'

Abby watched as Linda took the pan off the heat and turned off the gas.

'Isn't that a good reason to get a stable job?'

It was Aunt Linda's turn to roll her eyes as she turned to put the pan in the sink.

'No it's not. It's more of a reason to chase your dreams . . .'

'You think so?'

'I know so,' she said huffily. 'What about the Magic Triangle? He's been wanting to get in there since, well, forever.'

It was getting hot in the narrow kitchen now; the

steam from the pan had clouded up all the windows. Abby thought that she had a point there, actually. It had been one of Dad's dreams for as long as she could remember to be invited to be a member of the Magic Triangle, a highly secretive association for the best magicians. No-one even knew who they were, you couldn't ask for membership, they came to find you, if you were good enough. If you were extraordinary enough. Abby tried to stop her mind going back towards the shed, and the trunk and the book . . .

'Your mother wouldn't have liked it at all, that's all I'm saying.'

Abby was irritated now, by the heat, by Aunt Linda's bluntness, by everything.

'But she's not here, is she,' replied Abby, 'and nothing good ever came of magic for us . . .'

Linda looked hurt by that.

'He'll regret it, that's all I'm saying.'

Abby looked away.

Linda and Mum had become friends when they were around Abby's age. Linda was always playing truant and Mum missed a lot of school because her own mother was always travelling to perform, so they found themselves spending a lot of time in detention together, each one a kind of strange anchor to the other. A fixed mark when everything else was always changing. For Abby, Linda was like a memory bank of her mother that went way back to before she was born.

It was then that she shouted for Lenny, even though he'd come through to the kitchen, and was standing right behind them.

'LENNY!'

Linda's voice made Abby's ears ring.

'Blimey, Linda.'

'Sorry, if you don't shout, he doesn't hear you. He's in his own little world with his phone and his drawings.'

'Right, come on then, let's eat.'

Abby and Aunt Linda had hardly talked as Linda walked her home, but Abby wasn't worried. That was just Linda's way. Her anger would burn brightly before fizzling out quite quickly. She'd grabbed Abby and squished her into an unceremonious embrace like she usually did when they parted, before disappearing back into the twilight.

It was getting dark now so Abby lit the lamps and closed the curtains. Dad had been invited to go for a drink with Beverley, his new manager at the care home, and a couple of the staff, so he could get to know them a little. He had in fact been very excited about it, having not actually been out socially with new people for years and years. He had left her a note with three scribbled mobile numbers on it, in case she needed him, a sachet of posh hot chocolate and a pack of two shortbread biscuits, which he'd probably brought back from the care home. Abby smiled. Ta-da was scurrying around tonight so she whistled for him and lifted him out of the tunnel to carry him to the bed . . .

. . . and it was then . . .

. . . that she saw it . . .

The book.

Lying on her pillow.

Abby froze. She blinked and looked again. It was there. She found herself putting Ta-da down on the bed without taking her eyes off it.

She had that weird feeling again. It was impossible. She had put it back into the trunk. She had closed it.

She had shoved it out of sight and out of mind. Yet here it was. Over the past few days Abby had tried to push it out of her mind, yet somehow it found its way back in. Like pushing a ball underwater, the harder she shoved it down, the stronger it would pop back up. And here it was. Abby picked it up. She thought of the way those words, the ink, just seemed to move on the page. Like starry inky mercury pulled by some magnetic force into letters and words she didn't understand but felt like she knew. She picked it up, opened it once again, flicked past the title page to the first section, to the pages edged in gold. And there were the symbols. Exactly like before. The trembling came back in the pit of her stomach, but she wasn't scared or worried this time. It was like it was inevitable. Something that she had to go through.

She looked at the symbols. Watched as the intensity of the ink grew. Darker, darker. More fluid. And then, the same dizziness, the same sense of being unsteady. The edges on the symbols began to bleed. To move. The words shifting and settling into new arrangements. She didn't close it this time, she breathed deeply and let it happen. Vowels. Consonants. Words forming. Reforming. 'Lapina . . .'

She studied it again.

'Lapina . . . levati . . . nevaro.'

She felt her body relaxing as the words started filling her up.

'Lapina . . . levati . . . nevaro . . . liventium.'

Their familiar sounds in her ears. Then, and only then, did she look up and see Ta-da rising up off the bed, his paws dangling limply, looking at her in a surprised way. Up and up he went, casting a shadow on the wall behind him and he kind of hung there. Abby blinked and watched him open-mouthed as he spun slowly in the

chink of light that came in through the closed curtains, his fur beautifully white like a little rabbity cloud. It was like time had stood still. It was impossible. It was utterly and totally impossible, but there he was, hanging in the air, looking entirely astonished. Abby laughed. She laughed and laughed and took her eyes off the book, at which point Ta-da started falling back onto the bed. She dived towards him, caught him and pressed him to her. She stood up, her heart in her mouth, her voice strangled. She started to laugh again. She laughed and she laughed until her stomach ached.

CHAPTER TEN

Abby woke up squinting. There was a noise outside and a crick in her neck. She got up, her nose wrinkled and she rubbed the side of her neck. Dad was rattling around outside. It was then that she came to and remembered. The book! Ta-da! She'd waited up for Dad until really late, desperate to tell him everything but she must've gone to sleep . . . She pulled on a jumper, checked on Ta-da after his aerial adventures and ran outside.

Dad had just finished putting the pigeons into the basket on the front of the tandem.

'Morning sunshine,' he beamed, 'I thought we'd take them for a flight!'

He closed the leather buckle on the wicker basket and wheeled it towards Abby.

'I'm so sorry I was late last night,' he said leaning

the bike on the side of the bus.

'Dad, I need to tell you something . . .'

'Ok my lovely, but we really need to get going,' he said, passing her and disappearing into the bus, 'it's supposed to rain this afternoon.'

The pigeons were cooing in the basket, impatient for their flight.

'It's important!' said Abby.

'Absolutely. You can tell me on the way,' came his muffled voice. He returned with a paper packet. 'I've made us some jam sandwiches.' He kissed her head. 'Get your trainers on,' he said looking worriedly at the sky. 'Is it starting to spit?'

Abby rushed back onto the bus to pull on her trainers. Then she tipped the schoolbooks out of her rucksack and shoved the spell book into it. She tied it quickly and pulled the straps around her shoulders.

Every weekend, usually on a Sunday after a show, Abby and Dad would take the pigeons to stretch their wings. They had a tandem bike that Dad had rescued from a skip somewhere. It had once been a flash shade of red but Dad had repaired it, and had a go at painting it blue with an extremely optimistic yellow lightning rod along the frame. It always made Abby giggle, because lightning-fast it was not. Dad handed Abby her helmet and she squished it onto her head and clicked the strap before jumping on the back of the bike.

Dad pushed off with his leg and off they went. It had been a struggle at first to ride the tandem together, but slowly, as Abby's legs got longer and could pedal better, they learnt to work together instead of against each other and things had improved. It had become so natural they never even thought about it now.

The pigeons were homing pigeons. Abby had learnt that from the man they bought them from. Basically, from what Abby gathered, when the pigeons were young, they would fly up into the air and make a kind of map. They'd fly round and around, taking in every building and every tree and build up a kind of chart in their mind and at its centre was home. After that, they could go anywhere in the world. Miles and miles away, and they'd always have a feel, an instinct for home. Abby envied them for that. She had felt that at ease once, with Mum. An instinct, a kind of pull towards a centre. Even though she loved Dad with every inch of herself, her sense of home had been complicated when Mum died. It wasn't so simple anymore.

The pigeons needed to exercise their own instincts sometimes, so Abby and Dad would cycle miles away and set them free before racing them home. They never won of course. Pigeons were super-fast flyers when they got going and Dad and Abby and the blue thunderbolt just couldn't compete.

Dad was huffing and puffing loudly as they cycled up the hill towards the road that led into the lanes above the town. They would stretch for miles in a zigzag of country lanes that seemed endless. There were a million crossroads and very few signs. If you weren't local, or a pigeon, you'd get lost in an instant.

Abby felt the sun warming above them, the sea glistening down below as the first tourists had started coming. She could also feel the book on her back as she rode. She'd tell him once they were there. Once they'd let the birds go. That's what she'd do. Abby and Dad concentrated as the cycling became harder, the silence only broken by the rustle of wings against wicker and the scrabbling of claws.

At around eleven, they arrived at a new field, one they hadn't released the pigeons in before. The idea was to try and confuse them. Give them a new route to figure out. Occasionally, the odd one would get lost and get home long after the others had been shut away, and once a pigeon had even returned two days late, looking a bit sheepish; but most of the time, they'd be there, waiting for them when Abby and Dad pulled up exhausted from pedalling the bike.

Dad got off the bike to open the gate and Abby followed suit, removing her helmet. Dad walked the bike to the middle of the field and pulled off the basket.

'Blimey,' he said breathing heavily, 'that was hard. He leant his hands on his knees to catch his breath. Abby watched him.

'Dad . . .'

Dad put his hand up.

'Hang on a minute.'

Abby waited for him to get his composure and straighten up.

'Wooooooo!' he exclaimed as his breathing settled.

'Who's ready for some water and a jam sandwich?'

They sat in the long grass, as the sun started climbing the sky, and shared a bottle of water and some sandwiches.

'I think I've found a buyer for the magic stuff,' he said, brushing away the crumbs around his mouth with the back of his hand.

Abby raised her eyebrows.

'Turns out Tony knows the guy who runs the pier. He needs some props or something.'

'There's no need to, Dad.'

Dad looked at her.

'Listen, I know it's hard to let go but they're just things.'

'I know that, but I need to tell you something . . .'

Just then, a wing poked out of the basket and all hell broke loose inside. Dad jumped to his feet.

'What on earth is going on in there? Ok, ok—' he tried to comfort the pigeons – 'let me set you free . . .'

Despite her frustration, Abby loved this bit. Dad whistled softly to them and then undid the leather strap smiling over at Abby.

'One, two, three!' He lifted the basket lid. The burst

of energy was instantaneous, a shock of feathers. They flew upwards, defying gravity, and found a path to the sky. Their greyness now blending into the sky, and their clumsy wings suddenly sharp and elegant. Abby watched, her heart beating a little faster. She looked up as they soared, a certain heaviness in the pit of her stomach. A yearning that felt a little like envy.

'Come on then,' said Dad, brushing himself off and attaching the basket to the tandem once more.

'Sorry, Abby, the sandwiches and chat will have to wait!'

Abby looked up before pulling her helmet back on. She slung her rucksack on her front this time.

'Let's race them!'

'Dad?'

'Come on!'

He'd already climbed on so she jumped on the back as he turned the bike towards the gate. The trip home would be faster since it was more downhill. Dad seemed to be determined and was pedalling faster. But Abby couldn't wait any longer.

'Dad!' Abby shouted.

'Yes?'

'I found something.'

'Can you see them? The pigeons?'

'Dad, I found something in the shed.'

'Ok . . .'

The wind was rushing past them now as they cycled down a long hill.

'It's a book.'

'Abby, I can't see them anywhere. Did we lose them already?' he shouted.

'IT'S A SPELL BOOK!'

'Oh thank goodness, they're over there,' he said.

Abby felt her frustration bubbling up, she yanked the book out of her bag, opened it in the middle section and, balancing with one hand, started staring at the words. She was out of breath now, the heat flowing through her body. She tried to steady her gaze, tried to make out the words, and then it started happening. The ink started moving and the words appeared.

'Binuo . . . en . . . Binuo . . . enchanta . . . libre . . .'

She whispered the words, her breath short.

'They're leaving us behind,' shouted Dad.

Abby wasn't listening, she was concentrating.

'Biuno . . . enchanta . . . libre . . .'

It was then that the tandem seemed to pluck underneath them as if a bolt of electricity had shot through it. A light flashed and the tandem started going faster and faster.

'Abby, what are you doing?' came Dad's voice.

'It's not me, it's the spell book.'

'What spell book?'

'The one I was just telling you about!'

At this, the bike started jolting and suddenly Abby felt like they were a little further from the ground.

'Abby. ABBY!' shouted Dad. 'What's happening? What's happening Abby!'

The bike was taking off, it was flying. Up and up it went. Hedge-high to start with, then pylon high and then they were above the trees, the greenery flashing below them.

'Abby, what on earth?!'

'I've been trying to tell you!' shouted Abby. 'It's a spell book, a real-life spell book.'

'We're FLYING, Abby!'

'I found it in Grandma's trunk.'

'Abby, this is RIDICULOUS.'

'I know.'

'IT CAN'T BE HAPPENING!'

'I KNOW.'

Just then, they heard the beating of wings. It was the pigeons. All around them. Dad looked over at one, and it looked back incredulously, and Dad started laughing. He laughed and he laughed and raised his hands above his head like he was on a rollercoaster.

'WAAAAAAAAAAAAAAHHHHHHHHEIIIIIIIIII!' he screamed, his heart bursting with joy. Abby laughed,

95

then raised her hands too, making sure to grab hold of the book tightly, and they sailed past the pigeons.

'SO LONG, SUCKERS!' laughed Dad.

They flew higher over the hill behind the town, the tandem's wheels still turning. The wind was rushing through their hair and, for the first time in a long while, both of them felt alive. Really alive. The air felt new in their lungs and the excitement was bubbling in their veins. The bike flew back towards the bus, and Abby could see it, a little blue rectangle in the distance. It looked so small from here. The world so big. The town below like a little model.

Abby turned to see the pigeons catching up with them.

'They're coming, Dad,' shouted Abby, 'they're coming!'

Abby and Dad started pedalling to see if that would make them go faster. It did and they pulled away once again, the sound of wings retreating behind them.

'I hope our dodgy brakes hold out,' Dad half-joked as they got nearer and nearer, and lower and lower.

Abby hadn't thought of that.

'We're going a bit fast, Abbs!'

He was right. The ground was approaching quickly. Everything looking bigger and bigger and then they were only metres from the ground, then half a metre and the bike tyres were brushing against the tall grasses in the field. The bike touched ground and as it did, it started skidding towards the bus and the shed. Dad pressed the brakes but there were none, really, so the bike started shunting sideways and skidded into the shed. Suddenly there was a poof of dust and a deathly silence. Then came the sound of Dad's laughter. Abby tried out her limbs. She'd landed in a knot and wanted to check if anything was broken. She got up slowly. Dad was still laughing, his face incredulous. He took off his helmet and threw it on the ground.

'That,' he said, 'was PHENOMENAL. WOO HOOOOOOOOOOOOOOOOOOOOOOO!'

He was jumping up and down now. He ran over and grabbed Abby, his eyes on fire.

'This is TERRIFIC!' he laughed. 'This is UNBELIEV-ABLE! You have got to tell me ALL about it!'

Then he hugged her and they both screamed. He did

a mixture of dancing and whooping and giggling until they noticed that the pigeons had finally arrived back. They landed, one after another, and looked at Dad and Abby dancing and kicking up dust in the shed.

CHAPTER ELEVEN

Dad still hadn't calmed down. It was ten at night now and Abby had talked him through where and when she'd found the book. He'd walked up and down the shed, almost bouncing with adrenaline. He looked at the book, back and front. Opened it. Closed it. Turned it over and upside down. He'd never seen it before, and was sure that Mum hadn't mentioned it in all their years together. After coming into the bus, closing the curtains and switching on the lamps, they sat at the table and she tried to tell him how it worked. 'There was a message at the beginning of the book,' Abby said trying to control the excitement in her voice, 'I was looking at it, and these words appeared, I couldn't believe it. I thought I was imagining things.'

Dad listened enraptured.

'It said that there were three types of spell that we can learn, practise, but that once we perform them in front of others, they disappear.'

'Three spells?' he asked.

Abby nodded.

'The first must be levitation because I levitated Ta-da.'

'You levitated Ta-da?!' gasped Dad.

'The second must be a flying spell . . .'

'The tandem . . .' Dad caught on.

'I have no idea what the last kind might be,' said Abby.

Dad was trying to take it all in.

'So, explain it to me again,' he said, 'you get a funny feeling?'

'Yes,' replied Abby, 'and then the words start forming and it's like the spell appears.'

Abby pushed the book towards him.

'You try.'

Then she watched as he concentrated hard on the letters to see whether he could make the spells appear himself, but despite trying again and again, the words would just not reveal themselves to him. The letters stayed solid. The ink, impervious. The symbols stayed apart. Then he looked up at her in wonder.

'Well, isn't that just marvellous?' He had a wide grin, a strange pride on his face. He put the book down and rubbed his hands together.

'You know what this means, don't you?'

Abby shrugged.

'You and I, for some weird and inexplicable reason, have stumbled upon a bit of real magic. Real magic, Abby! And the magic seems to have chosen you to unlock it.'

He got up, tapping his chin.

'I've heard of this before. It's like the stars need to align, it's like the magic needs to find the right person and, poof! It's wondrous . . .'

'The thing is,' continued Dad, 'we've been playing around with illusions, with tricks, but this . . . this . . .' he said again, 'is real.'

The way Dad said 'real' this time sent shivers down Abby's spine.

'If you wanted to, we could do things, show things to the world that have never been seen before.'

Abby thought about this a moment.

'I mean, for every million illusionists, there's one who's

got access to real magic.' His eyes were drawn to the old posters glimmering now in the lamplight. 'Those people, Houdini, Thardo, they had it. They were the greats and now you—' he sat down again and held her hands – 'my precious girl, have been given this wonder . . .'

'We've been given this wonder,' Abby corrected him.

Abby felt a nervousness deep down inside. The start of something. She had no idea why she had been chosen by the book, but the more she held it, the more connected she felt she was. Dad was looking at her now, a sudden seriousness on his face.'

'Three spells, Abby! You'll have to start thinking about what you want to do with them,' he said beaming proudly.

'Erm, we'll have to think about what do with them, you mean?'

'The possibilities are endless,' he smiled, his eyes lighting up.

'And it would be a shame to keep them for ourselves,' added Abby.

Dad smiled at her.

'You are absolutely right. Goodness knows, there are plenty of people who could do with a little bit of magic, eh?' he said, clapping his hands with glee.

Abby could tell his mind was already buzzing. Then, he looked at her, suddenly serious.

'The only thing is, we have to keep this a secret. The book. For now anyway . . .'

'Of course,' nodded Abby.

'It's precious, we need to be careful with it. It belongs with us now, but it's also more than us.'

Abby could see that he was serious, then his face broke out into a smile.

'Now put it back by your bed and I'll make us some food.'

Abby reached out and found that the book was starting to feel familiar in her hands. Like it was becoming part of her.

'You actually hungry?' asked Dad, his mind still elsewhere.

'No,' Abby replied.

Dad smiled at her. 'Me neither.'

*

The next morning, they got up extra early. They ate some toast and butter and scraped the tandem off the shed floor. They dusted it down, straightened the front wheel a little and Dad fixed the brakes. Abby placed the book in her rucksack, and they cycled off into the hills. They needed a large open area to work where they wouldn't be seen. They pedalled in silence, both thinking about what they were about to do and what they might find out.

Behind the field they had used to set the pigeons free last night there was a woodland. The leaves had broadened out now and provided good cover. They left the tandem by the fence and Dad gave Abby a leg over the barbed wire into the woods. She landed on the other side and watched as Dad performed some kind of kung-fu move which saw him half-jumping, half-falling and landing on his bum on the other side, after which his head popped up like a meerkat with an 'I'm ok'.

They walked deeper into the woods and found a clearing. Abby leant the rucksack against a tree and pulled the book carefully out of the bag. Neither of them knew what was about to happen, if anything at all. Dad was pacing around a bit trying to contain his apprehension, desperate to help Abby learn more about the book.

'So,' asked Abby breathlessly, 'how should we do it?'

Dad shrugged. 'I don't know,' he said. 'The same as you did before, I guess . . . But don't force it, just go with the flow?'

Abby nodded and opened the book at the last section, noticing her palms were sweaty. She breathed heavily and tried to relax her shoulders a little. 'Ok,' she nodded, and opened the book. 'Ok,' she said again.

She tried to concentrate, but Dad's hovering presence was putting her off. She centred herself again and took a few deep breaths. She looked at the symbols. Let her eyes bring them in and out of focus for a while . . .

'Anything yet?' her dad piped up.

'No, Dad,' she replied, 'I'm trying to concentrate.'

'Oh, sorry.'

Abby refocused. Looked at the curves of the symbols. The dots. The letters that she still didn't know what they . . .

'What about now?'

'Daaaaaad!'

'I'm sorry, I'm excited, that's all,' he said, fizzy with fidgeting.

Dad made a zip motion across his mouth with his hand. He moved out of her eyeline just in case he distracted her further.

It was getting warm already, the trees casting dappled light around them. Abby looked back at the book. The sun was playing on the surface, making the symbols drift in and out of the shadows. She cleared her throat and looked back down . . . and waited and waited . . . and then, slowly, the dizziness came, except it wasn't quite a dizziness this time, but an excitement. Her eyes were glued to the page and, sure enough, the ink started to flow. It bubbled up and moved . . .

'Patreo . . .'

The second word was forming slowly.

'Patreo . . . vacuum.'

Abby said the words out loud.

'Patreo . . . vaccum . . . libro.'

She looked up. Nothing was happening. She was sure that's what it had said. She looked at the words again. They were clear as day.

'Patreo . . . vaccum . . . libro.'

Her heart was beating painfully now. Her breathing fast.

'Nothing's happening,' she said, and turned to show Dad when she noticed he wasn't there anymore.

Abby's stomach lurched.

'Dad? Dad!'

But there was no sign of Dad and no noise except for the rustling of the leaves and her own breathing. She turned in a full circle and shouted.

'DAD! DAD! Where are you?'

She looked back at the book. The words had disappeared and the symbols were back. What had she done? She ran into the middle of the clearing. Swung around. She could feel her chest pounding. Her mouth dry.

'Dad!' Her voice sounded small and strangled in her throat. He was gone. He was utterly and totally gone.

'HOLY MACKEREL!'

Abby almost jumped out of her skin. She turned around. He had appeared right behind her.

'Well that was unexpected.'

'DAD!'

Abby turned and grabbed onto him.

'What on earth happened there?'

'I thought you were gone.'

Dad laughed a moment, 'WHEEEEW! So did I for a bit!'

Abby's face softened and she thumped her dad jokingly on the arm, then they both started laughing. Laughing and laughing with relief and joy and excitement.

'That was phennooooommmmmmenal,' he shouted.

The day passed in a whirl of experimentation. They worked through the sections of the book and found that there were only three basic types of spells – levitation, flying and disappearing. The first third of the book with pages edged in gold were levitation spells. Each page was covered in symbols but as Abby flicked through them, she would be drawn to one of the spells and as she concentrated on it, the ink would start to move and form magical words which seemed to describe the object she was working the magic on. Every time she tried one, she could gently lift just about anything she wanted to off the ground and hold it there for as long as she concentrated. If her mind started to wander, the object would drop suddenly from the sky.

The middle section, with pages edged in silver, was full of flying spells which worked basically the same way. She would be drawn to a spell, and it would give her the words she needed to make the object she wanted fly. Abby had worked out that the smaller the object, the faster it flew and that if she kind of kept her mind on an end point, she could sort of control the direction of whatever was flying. The disappearing spells in the third section with the copper edging were a bit trickier. The bigger the object, the harder it was to disappear it. Rocks, flowers and bugs were easy, Dad was harder to keep invisible for a long time and trees were almost impossible although she could get them to look a little see-through.

Dad had spent most of the morning running around the clearing shouting, 'Try this! What about this?' as they tried to get to grips with exactly what the magic could do and how to use it.

At lunchtime, they sat tired and happy and shared some sandwiches that Dad had made from the crusts of the sliced loaf. They had a flask of squash and they both sat looking up occasionally at the blue sky through the burgeoning canopy. The light was dazzling above them and they listened to the birds for a moment. After eating, Dad tried to get her to think really hard about things. Like a rose or a dog. Anything. To see if she could make them appear, but there was nothing. It seems she could only work with things that were there. Present. She couldn't create anything, or bring things to her. Dad hugged her then, and they finished their flask of squash, both of their unspoken thoughts centring on Abby's mother.

By the end of the day Dad was all bumps and bruises, having flown, hovered and been disappeared several times. It was getting dark and they still had to cycle all the way back to the bus. Abby put the book back in the rucksack and sighed as they walked back towards the tandem. She was exhausted. Her dad came over and hugged her before putting her helmet back on her head.

'Don't fancy flying us home?' he asked.

'Er, no,' she replied. 'We need to be careful, remember? We don't want to draw too much attention, do we?'

'Good point, well made,' he laughed, and kissed her head.

'This has been the best day ever,' he said. Abby smiled.

'It has been great, hasn't it?'

They got back on the tandem and rode back towards the town. The stars had come out above them and there was a lovely coolness in the air. All the way home, they laughed and joked in the way they used to when Abby was younger, and when they got back to the bus, they made hot chocolate, brought out two chairs and lit a fire in an old metal tyre. Together they watched as the moon rose resplendently into the sky.

CHAPTER TWELVE

Myra had been working for hours. She put a chair under the doorknob so no-one could barge in and her paper patterns were all over the floor. She was so determined to get the dress right that she had unpicked every stitch she had made, pulled apart every seam and had started again from scratch. She pinned the pieces all back together and started to sew them loosely in place, not quite having the confidence to stitch them firmly in case she made yet another mistake. Her fingers were aching as she sat at her desk trying to wrangle the material.

The scrape on her cheek had scabbed over. She told her parents that she'd tripped and fallen, although to be honest she knew that her mum didn't believe her. Mum seemed to have superhero senses that could hear you eating snacks on your bed before dinner, even with the door closed, and she also always knew when Myra was lying, which she would communicate with a slight narrowing of her eyes. She'd dabbed the scrape with some stinging antiseptic waiting for Myra to tell her what really happened. Myra had thought about phoning Abby to tell her too, but she wanted to tell her face-to-face. To be honest though, there was something bigger preoccupying her. She sighed and looked again at the dress.

What hurt Myra the most was not being called a weirdo. She was used to that. It wasn't even the scraped cheek, although that had stung. It was just that Jasmine's words usually rolled off her like water off a duck's back. When her sewing was going well, Myra didn't really care what anyone said about her work. It felt easy to ignore nasty comments when she knew deep down that they were absolute nonsense, but now Jasmine's jibes felt different. Myra just didn't feel so tough, so bulletproof. Sewing and designing had always come so easily to her, so this new feeling of not quite being able to nail it was new to her, and she really didn't like it. It was a bit like starting to learn a new language and then finding out that you didn't have the words for the things you wanted to say.

She tried to stitch on the sleeve once again and found her fingers tangling in the thread. She groaned and pulled her hand free, but as she did so, because the material was so thin, the dress ripped all the way down the back. Myra looked on aghast. All that work! She felt her temper rise and pulled at the rip in frustration, listening to the cotton tear apart. She yanked the sleeve off and then the skirt, the thread releasing a white fabric dust into the air. She pulled and pulled, her shoulders and fingers aching, until there was nothing but a pile of rags in front of her. Then, she got up and marched the torn remnants of the dress to the bin. She stood breathing heavily before turning back towards her bed, when something caught her eye. The wardrobe door was open, and there were all the clothes she had customized. She looked at them, her heart sinking. Perhaps they were stupid. Perhaps dreaming of being a designer was stupid. Perhaps she had to face that she wasn't good enough and that she'd never be good enough.

Suddenly, she stomped over and pulled out an old suitcase, which lay at the bottom of the cupboard. She picked it up and threw it open on the bed. Then she turned, grabbed all her clothes off their hangers and threw them into the case. Garment by garment, bundle by bundle, until all that was left in the wardrobe were the few 'normal' clothes that she had. She zipped the case shut and and shoved it under her bed.

Afterwards, she pulled off the skirt and shirt she was wearing, and pulled on a bog standard pair of blue jeans and a T-shirt. Myra thought they felt scratchy. The denim was stiff and restrictive, the T-shirt, too high on her neck. She closed the wardrobe door and looked at herself in the full-length mirror on the other side. She looked different, that was sure, but maybe that wasn't a bad thing. Maybe Jasmine was right.

'Myra?' There was a knock at the door. Myra jumped up and quickly moved the chair that was blocking the door. She opened it. Her mum was standing there looking a little unsure.

'There's . . . There's a friend waiting for you downstairs . . .'

Her mum looked at her dad who had gotten up and was standing watching her.

'If it's Abby, tell her to come up.'

'It's not Abby,' they said. Myra was confused. She walked towards the top of the stairs and made her way down into the shop. She peeked down to see who was there and saw a pair of trainers and jeans. It was Josh. She frowned, continued down the stairs. He was looking at some of the clothes so that he hadn't even noticed she was there. Myra cleared her throat. He almost jumped out of his skin.

'Oh! I'm sorry,' he said, turning to face her. Myra stood barefoot at the bottom of the stairs. He took in her jeans and T-shirt.

'You look, er . . . different,' he said.

Myra didn't know how to answer that. 'Look, if you're here to be mean, you can just get—'

'No, no. It's not that . . .'

They stood in awkward silence for a moment. Josh hardly looking at her through his heavy fringe. He seemed to be concentrating hard on his own trainers. He looked smaller now that he was on his own. Younger almost.

'I . . . I . . .' he started and then stopped. Myra raised her eyebrows in anticipation of him saying something.

'I just wanted to say that Jasmine shouldn't have pushed you.'

Myra didn't know what to say. He never stopped them saying anything. He never said anything, in fact. And to Myra, people like that were as bad as the bullies themselves. He looked really uncomfortable now. He pointed at her cheek.

'Is that getting better?'

Myra shrugged. She waited for him to continue the sentence, but his words dried up once again. Myra was getting remarkably annoyed.

'Was that all you wanted?' she asked. It was his turn to clear his throat now.

'I just wanted to say, you shouldn't listen to them . . . That's all.'

And then he nodded and turned away, leaving the door wide open as he exited the shop. Myra stood for a moment, thinking. Then she walked towards the door and locked it. She watched through the glass as he made his way down the street, his head down, as if talking to himself.

CHAPTER THIRTEEN

'Good morning, Sweetie Pie.'

It was Dad. He was sitting on the side of Abby's bed, bouncing up and down in order to wake her up.

'Wake up, wake up! Come on, there's cereal.'

Abby rubbed her eyes. He was already in his work uniform. She stretched for a moment before sliding out of her bed.

Dad was mixing two kinds of cereal into a 'cereal salad' as he called it. In other words, he was using up the dusty remnants of two packets. He sploshed some milk on it and turned to rummage for a spoon. Then he sat down to watch Abby eat.

'You not having any?' Abby asked.

'I can have breakfast at work,' he said.

Abby smiled and continued to eat, becoming increasingly suspicious of the way her dad was grinning at her.

'I've been thinking . . .'

Abby rolled her eyes, this phrase didn't usually end well with Dad, either. It was never, 'I've been thinking, let's go on a holiday', or, 'I've been thinking, forget your homework tonight'.

'What is it?' she asked suspiciously.

'Well,' he said, 'this first spell . . .'

'Yes . . .'

'Where better to do it than at the care home?'

Abby raised an eyebrow.

'They have a recreation hall, and activities every Wednesday. Chair aerobics and bingo and stuff like that. I was thinking we could put on a show for them.'

Abby ran through it in her mind.

'Actually, it's not a bad idea . . .'

'I know,' he said looking pleased with himself. 'I mean, they need entertainment, they get pretty bored, and the bonus is that their expectations won't be too high. Glenys said the last activity they had was making a vintage steam

119

engine coaster. It sounded like a right yawn-fest. Surely we'd be better than that!'

Abby smiled.

'I just think, you know, that if anyone needs a little magic in their lives then it's them . . . They deserve a little sparkle.'

'I think that sounds perfect,' said Abby.

'I'm glad you said that,' he said, sliding a piece of paper off the kitchen counter opposite and blu-tacking it to the bus window.

Ta-da had come to join them now, and Abby reached for him and put him on the table.

'I've been thinking. What we need to do is to go back to basics.'

Abby looked at him in confusion.

'Back to the basics of what made the great magicians great. Great magic doesn't just try and dazzle the mind, it fills up your heart.' Dad was getting misty eyed now.

Abby listened and tried to keep track of what he was saying, which is hard when you're eating cereal salad and have a white rabbit trying to steal your rice puffs.

'Do you understand?' he asked.

Abby nodded, then shook her head. 'No.'

It was then that he started to explain, sometimes pointing towards the paper tacked to the window in what must've looked like the world's weirdest board meeting.

'The reason Houdini hanging upside down in chains and escaping from them was so iconic was not because it was difficult or impossible.'

'No?' Abby frowned.

'No! It was because every man, woman and child watching wanted to feel free. They wanted to think that anything that held them in or held them down could be overcome.'

Abby considered this.

'Errr, I suppose that makes sense.'

'Herrmann the Great would catch a bullet shot at him in his teeth, and people would go crazy, not because it was so fast and so dangerous, but because they wanted to feel invincible too. Like nothing could hurt them.'

'I get it.'

'So what we need to do is find something that the people in the care home would really love.'

Abby pulled Ta-da towards her, and stroked his ears.

'Well, they'd probably love to feel young again?'

'Bingo!' Dad smiled.

'We need to give them something that makes them feel young, and now that we know what the book can do, we can work with it to create the magic.'

'So, what were you thinking?' asked Abby.

Dad winked and rubbed his hands together, 'Ha ha,' he said, 'I thought you'd never ask . . .'

CHAPTER FOURTEEN

The magic show was to happen in the back of the recreation hall where there were two doors out into the car park. Dad wanted her to see the space, so Abby went to work with him, and they called to collect Myra on the way. Dad had insisted that she come with them, though Abby had no idea why. Abby was desperate to ask Myra where she'd gotten the scrape on her cheek from and what on earth was up with the normal trouser-and-jumper combo she had on today, but Dad was there so she thought she'd better leave it for now.

The residents would be wheeled into the recreation hall around one, after their lunch and Dad hoped they wouldn't all have a snooze like they sometimes did because then they would have a full hour. An hour to amaze them. To shake things up. To try the book out for the first time in front of an audience and try not to hurt, maim or disappear anyone. Every time she thought about it, Abby began to sweat. They'd been practising the magic in the shed with an old shop mannequin and a chair, but so many things could go wrong.

Dad let himself into the care home with his swipe card and they walked down the hot, beige corridors, which smelled slightly of cleaning products. He nodded to people as they walked along, eventually leading Myra and Abby into a large room with a square of parquet floor in the middle and chairs all around.

'So,' said Dad, 'what do you think?'

Abby didn't know what to say, it wasn't exactly glamorous. What with the crochet throws over the chairs, the fake flowers in pots and an old piano.

'It's . . . er, it's cosy . . .' said Abby lifting her eyebrows at Myra.

'I'll be doing some close work first, some card tricks and the like. Maybe we'll bring Ta-da for the hat and rabbit and then we'll move on to a few more exciting things.

'Hang on,' said Myra, 'so you're back doing magic

again? I wondered what on earth we were doing here.'

He spun around and looked at her.

'You are absolutely right, my dear.'

Myra gave him a look that could only be described as confused relief.

'So you've got over the, you know, disaster.' She didn't actually say the word disaster out loud, she only mouthed it.

Dad grinned.

'What disaster? I don't know what you're talking about!'

Myra grinned back at him.

'Abby and I have devised a new way of working.'

She looked at Abby, noticing her blushing and shrugging her shoulders.

'We've devised a new trick that has never been seen before . . .'

Myra frowned. 'I don't mean to throw cold water on this, but isn't that what you said about the flying rabbit trick?'

Dad's face fell.

'Not to worry, my little pamplemousse. This time

125

—' Dad smiled – 'we have something truly amazing up our sleeves.' He tapped the side of his nose mysteriously and winked at her. He started walking up and down the recreation hall now, his mind whirring.

'We're going to need the person we'll be doing the magic on up front,' he said.

There wasn't a raised stage or anything so Abby couldn't see a problem.

'And you'll need to be right behind me.'

They watched as Dad walked around, a kind of electricity running through him.

'Ahem,' coughed Myra to get Dad's attention, 'and can I ask where I fit into all of this?'

Dad threw his arms in the air, 'Oh! I almost forgot.'

'It's just that, when our last show went wrong, my cape, my magician's cape was ruined.'

'You want me to fix it?' asked Myra.

Dad shook his head, 'I'm afraid it's too far gone for that. I know it's a big ask and we haven't got much time but . . .'

'You want a new cape?'

Dad shrugged.

'It's just that we all know how brilliant at sewing you are.'

Abby smiled at Myra, then noticed the slight panic on her face.

'Oh, I'm not sure I have the time and anyway . . .' Myra could feel Abby's eyes on her.

'I'm not doing as much sewing now . . .'

Abby looked at Myra in confusion. Dad looked at Abby, not wanting to press the point.

'We'd be really grateful but it's entirely up to you, we don't want to push you in to it.'

Myra nodded.

'Have a think about it, kid,' smiled Dad.

Abby and Myra watched as Dad ran through things, walking back and forth between the back door and the 'stage' and looking at what the lighting in the room had to offer. Afterwards, Dad took them to meet the residents.

'Hello there, young' uns.' It was Jamal.

Abby and Myra smiled at him and he invited them to play draughts while Dad finished his shift. Even though Jamal's mind was, in his own words, not quite what it once had been, he beat them both and then introduced them to Beryl when she had woken from a little nap in the comfy chair nearby. Although she was so old she could hardly walk anymore, she was very talkative. She told them that she used to be a ballroom dancer and had loved to dance with her husband at tea-dances in beautiful shimmering ballrooms with Wurlitzer organs and glittering mirror balls. Abby smiled when she said that they had danced together for over sixty years but that now she was all worn out.

'The thing about getting old,' she'd said conspiratorially, 'is that life gets boring. Make the most of it while you're young. Give yourself permission to be happy and enjoy it.'

Myra then talked with Glenys who told her that she used to live in London a long time ago and had not married as she'd been too busy with her business. Then Dad came to show them where the kitchen was so they could make everyone some tea. Abby watched as Myra lined up the saucers on the tray and slid the cups into them and waited for Dad to give them some space.

'So . . .' said Abby, pointing to Myra's cheek, 'are you

going to tell me what happened?'

Myra looked at the cups a moment, then shrugged.'I had a little run in with Jasmine.'

Abby's heart sank. 'I knew there was something. I always get suspicious when you get quiet.'

'She pushed me.'

Myra watched as Abby inflated with anger.

'It's ok, it's ok . . . I'm over it.'

'Over it?' Abby boiled, much like the kettle.

'I am! She's not worth it.'

Abby studied her, looking again at her outfit.

'Except she's gotten under your skin.'

Myra smiled sadly. 'Maybe a little bit.'

'Listen, Myra, whatever her problem is, it's her problem, not yours. I have no idea why she's taking it out on us, but you can't let her get to you. That is exactly what she wants.'

'That's what Josh said.'

Myra clocked the confused expression on Abby's face.

'Oh, he came to the shop. Said I shouldn't listen to them.'

Abby was surprised by this. 'Well, he's right . . .

Although he's got a bit of a nerve since he never does anything to stop them.'

They stood in silence a moment.

'Listen, if doing this cape is too much, don't worry about it if you're not in the mood. Dad will be fine in a suit.'

Myra didn't answer, she was deep in thought.

'Come on then,' said Abby gently, 'let's take this tea out before it gets cold.

CHAPTER FIFTEEN

Dad had started jogging. He'd gotten up early three times this week already and pulled on his weird 1980s trainers to go for a run. Well, perhaps not a proper run. Abby had watched him – it was more of a lolloping walk. He'd come home every time looking like he was about to have a heart attack. Then he'd lie in front of the bus like a starfish until Abby brought him a glass of water, which he proceeded not to drink but to throw over his own face.

'Good Lord,' came Linda's voice this morning, 'what on earth happened to you?'

Abby smiled as Linda looked down at Dad like something nasty she was about to step in. Dad pushed himself up onto his elbows.

'Do you like my new sporty look, Linda?'

'Ronald, you look like a right berk,' she said, and proceeded to make her way onto the bus to make herself a cup of tea. Abby laughed and waited until she came out again with a tray of mugs and started passing them around.

'So?' she asked. 'What's so important? I had three missed calls, Ronald.'

'Well, I . . .' then he looked at Abby. 'We . . . wanted to tell you something.'

Linda raised her eyebrows, 'Oh, here we go . . .'

Dad smiled at Abby.

'You were right about the magic.'

Linda watched him suspiciously.

'It's just, we've got some unfinished business with it, so we're getting back into it for a little while.'

Linda almost dropped her tea.

'Well, hallelujah, some common sense at last.'

'We've got some plans for this town, this place, I just wanted to apologize, that's all . . .'

Linda smiled.' So what was it that you wanted to say?'

Dad looked confused now, 'Well, I already said, I

132

was sorry . . .'

'No, the bit before that.' Linda was looking mischievous now.

'I said, I was wrong and you were right.'

Abby watched as Linda's shoulders broadened.

'I think that's the first time you've said that to me, Ronald.' She looked pleased, very pleased indeed.

'And now that we've established I was right all along . . . Can I ask why the change of heart?'

Dad looked over at Abby and smiled.

'Well, let's just say we've got our mojo back . . . We friends?'

'Course we are,' said Linda rolling her eyes, 'but do go and shower and change, you look like a sweaty bullfrog and you smell like a ferret.'

Linda stayed for tea and Abby always loved the way they were as a trio when she was around. The way Linda teased and insulted her father mercilessly, and the way she pottered around doing not much but quite a lot at the same time. She knew the place inside out, so no one ever had to explain where things were or how things worked. She just knew. Ta-da also liked her, although she never hugged him – she didn't like furry creatures because of all the hair, but she would still bring him carrot peelings. The best thing, though, were the stories she'd tell about Abby's mother without even really thinking. Like the time she casually mentioned Mum had a new scarf confiscated by a teacher and how they'd snuck in the window of the staff room to steal it back. They were just little bits of information, but Abby treasured each and every one of them.

As Linda set the table, she started to grill Dad about the trick they were going to do at the care home. Dad had been suitably vague, but it made Abby's skin tingle and even Linda could see that they were both excited by this new magic. Dad had brought some leftovers from the care home kitchen and they ate them with potatoes while listening to Dad talk about his new elderly friends, Jamal and Glenys and Beryl.

After supper, they watched as the sunset spread over the town below, touching the spires and towers and hotels with gold until it settled into a dappled darkness. It was late by the time Abby went to bed. Dad made her a balloon dolphin, or at least that's what she thought it was. He kissed her head and as he turned, he said, 'You'll need to think about what to wear, too.'

Abby looked at him puzzled.

'What do you mean?'

He turned the light off. 'For the performance,' he said.

Abby sat up.

'But I really don't want to be on stage much,' she said.

'I know, but we are a team. We have to work together, equally. Just like your mum and me. A dynamic—'

'—Duo,' Abby finished his sentence and smiled softly.

'Abby, I could never stand there taking the credit for your magic. If we're doing this, we're doing it together and it's going to be amazing,' he added and turned away.

CHAPTER SIXTEEN

Myra stayed downstairs to try and finish sewing the cloak. Ever since Abby's dad had asked her, she had tried really, really hard not to think about it, but despite herself, her brain had started fizzing with ideas. It was a favour really. A one off. Just about one of the simplest things she could make, and she really wanted them to be happy, so she'd been to the library to look at pictures of magicians' capes, just for some research, of course. She found that most of them were a fairly plain black with a red underside, just like Ron's old one. She'd looked through her stash of fabric and the 'not collected' rail and there was nothing red or black, so she needed to improvise.

She'd spent hours thinking about the effect she wanted to create, and longer hours sketching ideas until she settled on one. She made the collar to look like one large magic wand wrapped around the Great Ronaldo's neck. She found enough inky blue velvet material to make the cape itself, and onto that she had started to stitch silver sequin stars she'd cut from an old ballgown.

The body of the cape was cut out, but she couldn't quite attach it to the silk on the underside and the material was so slippy she kept missing the stitches. Her neck was sore, and her eyes were having difficulty focusing. It was almost like the universe was trying to tell her something. What with Jasmine teasing her about her clothing, and Mum and Dad saying that affording college would be difficult, and her own frustration with her work, she was beginning to think that maybe, just maybe, she should quit while she was ahead.

It was strange, she thought, as she threaded a needle yet again and started to sew on another star. The thing about dreams was that you didn't really know how much they lit up your night sky until they weren't there anymore. Like stars, Myra thought. You didn't notice they were there, until you looked up and suddenly, they'd disappeared behind a cloud, making everything flatter

and duller. Suddenly, a dark spot appeared on the fabric, and Myra found she was crying.

It was then that she heard footsteps on the stairs.

'Myra?'

It was Mum.

'What are you still doing down here?'

'Nothing,' replied Myra, her voice thick with tears.

'Myra? What have you got there?'

Her mum rushed towards her. 'What on earth's the matter?'

Myra's shoulders were shuddering and she couldn't speak. Her mum walked over and enveloped her.

'It's ok, my lovely. You cry, it's ok to cry,' Myra heard through her sobs, and over the next few minutes she felt her upset dissolve into her mum's arms. Deepa kissed her head and held her face.

'I can't do it,' she sobbed.

'Do what?' asked Deepa.

'I can't be a designer, I can't even make this cape.'

Her mum looked at her in confusion.

'It's for Ron, a magician's cape, they're going to do a few more shows and I said I'd try, and it should be easy, I mean it's the easiest thing in the world, but, it's like I've got all muddled and I can't do it anymore.'

Deepa let her catch her breath and pulled out a tissue from her sleeve for her. She kissed her and pulled up a chair to look at the stars on the countertop. Myra could feel her face all hot and blotchy. Deepa took her time, let Myra's breathing settle.

'Now listen, Myra. I'm going to tell you something I haven't told you before,' said Deepa, smiling, 'and because you're getting older, I'm going to be very honest.'

139

Myra studied her. She could feel her nose felt stuffy now.

'The thing is,' she said, 'the thing is . . . that you have never been very good at being young.'

Myra looked at her shocked.

'By the time you were four, it was like you were ready to get a job and move out. You were so independent.'

Myra laughed now.

'It was like your brain worked at a hundred miles an hour but you were too small to do the things you wanted to and you despised it. Got frustrated, and you hated asking for help. Do you know that I used to have to wait forty-five minutes every morning because you were determined to tie your own shoelaces?'

'I sound like a nightmare,' said Myra, smiling.

'You were an absolute nightmare,' agreed Deepa, taking her hand.

'Asking for help is not a weakness, Myra. It's a vital skill for you to grow into who you want to be.'

Myra nodded, wiped her nose again.

'Your confidence has been knocked, but that is normal, Myra, it isn't the end of the world.'

Myra nodded.

'There's being strong and then there's shutting people out,' she said, stroking Myra's hand. 'So, are you going to tell me what happened with your cheek?'

Myra's fingers went to her face unconsciously.

'Oh, no, that was . . . just some kids, they're a bit, you know . . .'

Deepa nodded knowingly.

'Need us to get involved?' Myra's mum asked.

'It's ok, for now anyway,' replied Myra.

Deepa nodded. 'Ok, I trust you, but make sure to ask if you need us to do something.'

Myra nodded and watched as her mum pulled the cloak towards her.

'So,' Deepa said, looking at the stitching, 'when do they need this by?'

'Tomorrow night.'

Deepa nodded. 'Ok then,' she said, picking up a needle and smiling, 'we'd better get cracking.'

It was then that Myra and her mum started work. The velvet beneath their fingers was rich and dark, and after a while, her father brought them tea. Then he stood and watched, keeping them company as Myra and Deepa started sewing the stars back into the sky.

Abby and Dad got up early. They spent the morning practising in the shed, then loaded the van with the magic hats and boxes and Dad's magic wand. He was very particular about his wands. He only had two, one that was given to him by an older magician years ago, in an old tradition which was supposed to keep magic going from one generation to the next, and one that he had received from Mum on their wedding day. He only brought that one out on very special occasions and he kept it next to his bed in a long shiny varnished box. That one was inscribed with a few words that made no sense to Abby. She'd asked her dad about them once, but he said he had no idea what they meant and all he knew was that the wand had come down Mum's side of the family.

They'd decided Abby would stand at the side of the stage for most of the act. They would set the recreation room up with a table in the front and a screen behind them. Abby would then help with Ta-da, handing him to Dad and putting him back in the little carrier behind the screen. Abby had asked whether she could just wear her jeans, and Dad had been happy with that. They went over how Beverley would introduce them, how they'd walk onto the stage and how Abby would put on an old CD player for the last trick. Then, Abby was supposed to slip behind the screen once again and use the magic book. After the show they'd take their bows. That was the plan anyway.

Every time Abby thought about the book, she felt really trembly inside. Despite her nerves, she'd really have to concentrate or the whole thing would be a disaster. She'd handed things to Dad before, made sure props were in the right place, but this time, the magic was down to her. Dad was steaming his top hat with an old iron, hoping it would pop back into shape – it still hadn't fully recovered from the drenching it got at the caravan park.

'Are you nervous?'

Dad was watching her.

Abby shrugged. 'It's just, what . . . what if it doesn't work?'

Dad's smile broadened.

'There'll be thirty people there, tops, and they'll all be rooting for us.'

Abby relaxed a bit and took a deep breath.

'It'll be alright,' he reassured her.

At that moment, there was a knock on the door. It was Myra. She entered the bus with a bag under her arm.

'Here she is!' said Dad warmly. 'Wow! You look tired my lovely. Are you alright?'

'I'm ok,' smiled Myra placing the bag on the table.

'Is that the cloak?' asked Dad.

Myra nodded and petted Ta-da who was sitting on the table. Abby watched as Dad opened the bag and pulled out the cloak. He stood a moment in absolute silence. Myra looked at him anxiously.

'I mean, I didn't have much time, or quite the right materials. I can change it if it's not what you were thinking . . .'

Dad was still quiet.

'Is it ok?' Myra asked again.

Dad was open-mouthed. He looked at the cape in his hands, unfolded it.

'Is it ok? Are you crazy? This is the most magical

144

wonderful spectacular magic cape I have EVER seen in my entire life!'

Abby looked at it in awe.

'Mum helped me,' Myra said, going back to pet Ta-da and trying not to blush. It was then that Dad picked her up and threw her in the air.

'Myra! You are a genius! It is BLOOMIN' MARVEL-LOUS!'

Myra was laughing now. Dad was jumping and whooping so Abby joined in as Ta-da looked on, thinking they'd all finally lost their marbles.

CHAPTER SEVENTEEN

Even though the care home was in town, it was good to get there early to set up. They sorted the table and the tablecloth and put the screen in place. They carried in the trick boxes and the wands and Abby had the book stashed and safe in her pocket. It was weird. Whenever she had it with her, it made her feel on edge, though not in a bad way, in an excitable way. Like her belly was tight as a drum.

They could smell the cottage pie and peas in the dining room and knew the audience wouldn't be long. Dad had performed in front of large crowds and small ones. There were certain tricks that worked better up close, like card tricks or mind tricks. There were others that were better as a spectacle, that were best viewed from afar to capitalize on the awe of them. Today's trick would be better close-up.

'Well, this is flash, isn't it?'

It was Aunt Linda with Lenny in tow. Dad had asked her to be there to give an honest opinion of the show. And if there was anything that Linda could do spectacularly well it was giving an honest opinion. Lenny nodded in Abby's general direction and grunted in what was his usual fashion these days before getting himself a seat from the stack of chairs at the back and pulling his phone from his pocket. Linda then helped them make two rows each side with plenty of space for the wheelchairs. By then the audience had started to trickle in. There were a few people that Abby had seen watching TV when she was last there, being wheeled in by their carers. Then, in came Jamal, walking with his stick, who gave Dad a fist bump, and then Glenys, who giggled like a schoolgirl when she saw Dad. Behind them came Beryl, leaning on her carer's arm, being walked slowly to her chair in the front row.

Linda went to sit next to Lenny as Dad and Abby left the room to prepare for the show. Dad threw the cloak around his shoulders, and it glinted spectacularly in the sunlight. He tied it around his neck. Then he checked his pockets for his wand. Abby watched him, his nervousness making hers bubble to the surface. They could hear Beverley introducing them. Her voice came wafting out of the door . . .

'We're so lucky to have such talented staff . . . It's wonderful to be able to introduce the Great Ronaldo and his daughter Abby-cadabra.'

'Oh my God, Dad, did you have to use that name?'

Dad made a 'what?' shrugging motion. He grabbed her arms and kissed her cheek and winked.

'Let's show 'em some magic.'

Abby followed him inside and her eyes ached for a moment as they adjusted to the darkness. The lights were off, but Abby could still see all the faces, even Myra's, who had snuck in right at the back and was giving them the thumbs up.

Dad started his spiel and then it was onto the first part of the show. He moved towards the front row and did a few card tricks. These didn't go down too well, as some of the audience didn't have their glasses. After that were handkerchiefs produced from thin air. Those got a few 'ooohs' and 'aaaahs', and Abby could definitely feel the crowd warming up. Then, disappearing coins and ten-pound notes. The carers were laughing now as Dad pulled ten-pound notes from their ears, only to make them disappear into the older residents' hands. Abby stood, watching, trying not to feel as awkward on stage as she felt.

Dad walked back towards Abby and winked at her. It was her turn to take part. She slipped behind the screen to where Ta-da sat in his cage and carried him around to Dad. Dad showed him to the audience and put him in a box. He waved his favourite wand and, of course, when he picked up the box again, Ta-da wasn't there. Everyone loved Ta-da, and because of that, everyone loved this trick. Then, Dad did a few more illusions, before taking off his top hat as if to take a bow, and there, under his hat, was Ta-da, blinking a little under the light. This set off a semi-rapturous applause. Even Tony, the taciturn caretaker had come in by now, and was standing at the back smiling.

Abby picked up Ta-da, took him behind the screen once more and closed him safely in his cage. It was time. She could hardly believe it. The show had flown by. She pressed the button on the music player and the CD whizzed into action. It was an old showtune called 'Dance with Me'. Abby snuck a look through the hole that Dad had drilled in the screen so that she could keep an eye on what was happening on stage. Then she picked up the book.

'Come dance with me my love . . .' went the song '. . . And then we'll feel forever young.'

Abby opened the book in the levitation section. One of the spells seemed to call on her. Then she started concentrating. Hard.

'Take me in your arms, sway with me tonight . . .'

It was actually quite hard to concentrate with the music so loud and so close. They hadn't practised with the song and she was beginning to feel that maybe that was a mistake. She studied the letters and then, slowly, she started to feel warm and dizzy.

Dad was dancing on the stage now. He was waltzing away elegantly on his own, and then he bowed to Beryl, who beamed up at him from her chair in the front. He reached out a hand to her as if inviting her to dance. Abby felt herself getting warmer and, slowly but surely, the letters began to move. 'Anci . . .' She squinted. 'Anci . . . danza . . . chirosa . . .'

She repeated the words over and over and then something incredible happened. As Dad held Beryl's hand, she started to rise out of her chair. She'd told Abby that she was so old and frail that she never walked far anymore, but now she was standing in front of Dad. Abby kept whispering the words while looking out at the stage. Then Dad, gently as anything, pulled Beryl closer and they started to sway with the music. Abby could see the other residents gasp. Beryl looked at Dad, her eyes shining. Then, in front of everyone, and despite the impossibility of it, they danced, Beryl's feet hovering a few centimetres off the ground. Beryl looking to all the world like the young girl she had once been. The carers and Beverley had tears streaming down their cheeks as Dad and Beryl danced beautifully. The spotlight was like a full moon and everyone had fallen silent.

It was then that Abby felt it in her body. The power of it. The magnificence of the magic filling her up. Tingling and travelling across her skin. She watched as an old woman who had seemed to be so old and so tired became weightless, youthful. Beryl's eyes were closed now, and she and Dad were cheek to cheek. Somehow Abby knew she wasn't really dancing with her father, but with another man, probably someone she had loved a long time ago. And then, as the music came to an end, Dad placed her gently back down in the chair.

Abby looked back at the book and instead of the ink returning to letters and symbols, this time, it faded away, leaving a completely blank page. Then she saw that all the levitation spells had vanished. Abby held her breath. There was not the loud applause that they had expected, but a stunned silence. A reverence. A feeling that they had witnessed something both magical and real. Something that had wordlessly spoken to each and every one of them. Tony was the first to start clapping, then Lenny, who had filmed it all on his phone, then Linda. The others followed suit as Beryl looked on, a lightness in her face. Dad looked back and nodded at Abby. Abby looked at the empty page a while, before Dad called to her again, and asked her to join him on the stage to take their bow.

CHAPTER EIGHTEEN

That night, when they arrived home, Dad chatted endlessly and excitedly like he used to do years ago. He walked back and forth, up and down the bus, laughing and smiling and going over every moment. Even Ta-da had looked pleased with himself. They stayed up really late talking about how beautiful Beryl had looked, and how they had both felt the magic fill up the room.

The following morning, Dad was humming to himself as he made toast while Abby sat at the table looking at the blank pages of the spell book in the first third of the book.

'Dad?'

'Mmm?' He looked over at her as he theatrically smeared a thin layer of margarine on the toast. He read the seriousness on her face.

'What is it, Abby?'

'Don't you think it's a bit sad?' she asked tentatively.

Dad came to sit opposite her, putting the plate of toast in the middle of the table between them.

'What's a bit sad?' he asked, biting the corner off his slice.

'That the spells disappear after they're shared?'

Abby watched him think a moment.

'No, I actually don't think it is. In fact, I would say that it is wondrous. Imagine, if magic was there for everyone all the time, it would cease to be . . .'

'Magic,' said Abby.

'Exactly!'

'Listen,' he said, 'I've had everything I have ever wanted in life: you, your mum. This, this is just the icing on the cake. Even if it doesn't last that long. Let's just enjoy it.'

Abby felt her throat tighten and the prickle of tears in her eyes.

'It was brilliant, though, wasn't it?' he said, his eyes still dreamy.

Abby looked at him. It was, it really was . . .'

'People need this, Abby. They need us. I thought maybe things had changed, but magic, magic is timeless. Ageless.'

He was right. Abby had seen little children squeal in delight over the years and she had seen it in Beryl yesterday. It seemed there was something in people that needed it. That craved it.

'When I see an audience leaning in like that, everything gets stripped away. Their problems, their worries, their defences, every challenge they're facing . . . and their hearts open, and they're ready to be dazzled.'

Abby leant over and touched his hand.

'Imagine if we could live our whole lives like that,' he said gently. 'So it looks like we have two spells left, so we'll have to make the most of them, do them justice. Make them count. The great magicians, they turned up in a town, made a mark and left. That was how it worked. That's what made them legendary . . . the stuff of dreams.'

It was then that they heard a voice.

'RONALD!'

Abby looked at Dad confused.

'RONALD!' the voice came again. Dad pulled back the curtain and then they saw Linda running up the hill. She was waving something. Dad frowned. 'What on earth is that strange woman doing?'

She was trying to run in heels, and after a long while, Dad and Abby saw her mouth incredibly rude words. Then she bent down, took off her shoes and sprinted over to the bus. She burst through the door, her chest heaving, her face all blotchy, brandishing a newspaper.

She came towards them, almost on her knees, like

someone lost in the desert collapsing in front of an oasis. She flung her arm over her head and slapped the newspaper on the table. She was gasping, the twenty cigarettes she smoked a day making her lungs wheeze away like an engine.

Dad picked up the paper, and there he was staring back at himself with the headline, 'MAGICIAN STEALS SHOW'. Dad showed Abby the front page. It was a still image from a video someone had taken. It was then that Linda's head popped up, her eyeliner all smudged and her blonde hair all skew-whiff.

'Lenny videoed it all, put it on the internet, it's been watched hundreds of thousands of times.'

Abby and Dad looked at each other.

'It's a sensation,' she gasped, 'it's amazing!'

Dad stared at the picture again before placing it down and looking up. 'Well, I'll be a weasel,' he said.

It was then that his phone started ringing. They all looked at each other before he reached out and picked it up. He cleared his throat, 'Hello? Yes . . .'

Abby and Linda watched as he got up.

'*The Times* newspaper? Really?' They listened as he

cleared his throat. 'No, it's ok, I mean, I suppose I have got five minutes to talk, yes . . .'

And that was how the morning went. One phone call after the other. Asking how they'd done it. How long he'd been doing magic. How long Dad had been working in the care home. How old Abby was, etc. Linda made tea all day and carried cups back and forth, listening and in her element. Lenny would call her every now and again to tell her how many more times the video had been seen, and in how many countries.

At lunchtime Linda and Abby made beans on toast, picking off the mouldy bits of bread that had sweated a little in the bag, and they sat around the table. Dad was deep in thought.

'I've been thinking,' he said, 'this whole thing is becoming huge . . .'

Abby and Linda stopped eating for a moment.

'We've had agents and managers on the phone this morning trying to sign us, and I'm starting to think that we will actually need someone to help us.'

Abby put down her knife and fork. 'But you've never had a manager.'

He wiped his chin with the back of his hand.

'But this is different, Abby.'

Abby wasn't sure about inviting someone else in, someone who would tell them what to do. Someone she didn't know. There was the book to think of. They only had two spells left and everything had to be kept secret.

'You know we're only back in the business temporarily,' said Dad.

Linda nodded.

'But we want to do two more shows, only two, like the greats, so we need someone who'll help us get the most out of them. What we need is someone who's ruthless. Someone who can get blood out of a stone, who's good with money. Someone we trust. Someone loyal who'll look after us. Someone with a killer instinct that makes a Rottweiler chewing a wasp look friendly. Someone quite frankly like Linda.'

Abby and Dad looked at Linda.

'Me?' she said, clutching her chest.

Dad nodded.

'Aww,' she said, her eyes starting to fill with tears,

'you say the nicest things.'

Abby grinned.

'What do you say?' asked Dad.

Linda raised her eyebrows.

'Twenty per cent of takings . . .'

Dad narrowed his eyes, 'Five per cent.'

'Fifteen,' countered Linda.

'Ten,' said Dad folding his arms, 'final offer.'

Linda spat on her palm and offered him her hand. Abby watched as they shook on it.

Then the phone rang again.

'We need a gig that's bigger, Linda, the biggest venue in town.'

Linda nodded and grabbed the phone. 'Let me at 'em.'

After lunch, Dad disappeared to town. Beverley always paid those who came in to entertain and even though Dad already worked at the home, she wanted to do the same for him. She gave him five new twenty-pound notes.

Linda spent the whole day on the bus, a pencil stuffed behind her ear, jotting things down on a piece of paper as she chatted away on the phone.

Dad came home with some sausages from the butcher, some fresh eggs, and three tins of discounted paint he had found in the hardware shop, and Myra in the passenger seat. Abby looked at him in confusion.

'I thought it was about time that the van had a little TLC.'

Abby smiled.

They then spent the rest of the day repainting the old van. Abby did the lettering as she was good with calligraphy, Myra did the fiddly bits around the mirrors because she was good at details and Dad did the main work of repainting the van a rich and deep blue. As they worked, they talked about how often Dad and Mum had gotten lost on their travels in the van. How often Abby's mum would overstuff the van with tricks, only to have the dodgy back door open on the way and spill magic props into the middle of the road. They worked until there were smudges of paint everywhere, in Abby's hair and all over Myra's hands. The last thing Abby did was repaint the magic wand and the swirl behind it. This needed a steady hand, and she bit her lip in concentration. Dad and Myra had both finished and were standing watching her. Abby finished eventually, her arm aching and her neck stiff. She stepped back and stood next to Dad who was standing cross-armed. The lettering was almost luminous in the half light. THE GREAT RONALDO!

Abby looked up at Dad and she was sure she saw his eyes darkening with tears.

'Well, that looks great,' said Myra smiling. Dad put his arms around them both.

'Right!' It was Linda on the steps.

'I've got you a night at the pier, five hundred pounds, which admittedly is not great, but you also get twenty per cent of ticket sales and your own green room. The top billing and a basket of fruit, chocolates and water.'

Dad looked at her, beaming.

'I'm working on a clothes allowance. They're being a bit sticky with that one at the moment but I'm sure they'll come around with a little persuasion.'

'You've got us a gig at the pier?!'

'Yup. Bank Holiday weekend.'

'That's amazing!'

'I know,' she said cockily, 'and I reckon, next time, I'll do even better.'

Dad started jumping up and down and Myra and Abby laughed together.

To celebrate, they lit the fire outside the bus and fried sausages and eggs. They ate and talked and laughed. The whole bus was lit up with on orange glow and reverberated with joy. Abby looked around as the night settled in and felt a warmth she hadn't felt in a long, long time.

CHAPTER NINETEEN

Early next morning, they went to scope out the pier pavilion together. The performance was only a couple of weeks away, and they wanted to know what kind of space they were working with. They walked through the archway, past the fruit machines and met the caretaker by the door. Abby hadn't been in there for ages. Years ago, Dad had told her that it had been used to host the 'bonniest baby' and 'knobbliest knees' competitions, then after that it had been a dance hall, a theatre, but at the moment it was only used for bingo sessions, since nothing else brought out the crowds anymore.

The caretaker pushed open the doors with a great echoey clunk and Abby gasped. It was enormous. A huge space with a balcony all around. The ceiling was so high and the old curtains were still velvety and lustrous. Myra and Abby walked in, speechless, and heard their footsteps echo around the pavilion. They looked back at Dad who was standing there open-mouthed and slightly paler than he was before. He cleared his throat.

'It's bigger than I remember,' he said.

He turned in a circle looking around.

'So, how many bums on seats can we get in here?' Linda asked the caretaker, pulling the pen from behind her ear and starting to sketch the size of the place on her paper pad.

'A thousand,' he said before laughing, 'but don't get your hopes up, love, we've had nowhere near that for years. You're lucky if you get sixty into anything these days.'

Linda looked at him and narrowed her eyes.

'Really?' she said.

'Don't go getting any grand ideas, sweetheart,' he said again. Abby winced. She knew that look. The poor man had no idea what was coming. Abby watched as Linda squared up to him and she felt Myra take cover behind her shoulder.

'A,' she said pointedly, 'Don't you ever underestimate

165

me, and B, naysayers like you are what's wrong with this world. You automatically accept defeat and when things are difficult you think "Why me?", whereas people like me think, "Try me".'

Abby watched as he started to back away slowly.

'Oh, and C. Call me sweetheart or love one more time and you will seriously regret it, ok?'

He nodded, shaking. Linda looked at him sourly and said, 'I think we're fine by ourselves. We'll call you when we're done.'

Myra giggled as they watched him back away, as if scared to turn his back in case she jumped on him like a lioness on a scrawny elk.

Then there was the silence as Dad took in the space.

'Anything we do here will have to be big. To fill this space. So that people can see us at the back.' He was preoccupied now. Deep in thought.

Abby nodded. It was a beautiful building with cream arches and golden painted cherubs playing harps and bugles, and angels with their palms pressed together in prayer.

'Come on,' said Dad, 'let's look at the stage.' Linda

and Myra had gone to check out the green room.

Abby followed Dad all the way to the stage and climbed up the black stairs at the side. It was a deep stage with a few steps up the front. Their footsteps echoed around as they walked and Dad shouted out, 'I am the Great Ronaldoooooooooooooooo!' to test out the acoustics. Sound carried really well in here. That wasn't always the case. Abby had seen places where the theatres or halls were so badly designed that sound would be dampened, and then you'd need microphones and speakers, but here you could whisper, and it would carry around the balconies. It had obviously been designed and built by someone who knew what they were doing.

Dad stood, waiting for his voice to fade away. Abby went to stand by him.

'Did you know that this was the place I first met your mum?'

Abby felt something like electricity jolt her.

'I didn't know that.'

Dad smiled and looked down at her.

'We were just kids, not much older than you are now. She was doing a puppet show with your grandmother and I—' He shrugged. 'She was magnetic, and even though I was supposed to be looking at the puppets, all I could see was her.'

Abby felt her heart swell. Dad and Abby didn't talk much about Mum anymore. When she first died, they talked about her all the time, they'd been open and honest about everything. It was just that, after a while, and because she was gone, Dad had run out of new stories to tell Abby about her. That was the problem when someone died, they were missing from their own story, so slowly, and over time and with nothing new to say, Abby and Dad had reached a kind of silence about Mum.

'Your grandmother did the Punch and Judy on the promenade and then they moved in here for a while. I never had any money so I'd sneak in for the second half because no-one checked your tickets after the interval.'

Abby smiled.

'And then, I'd wait by the stage door, every night. Me and Mum would sneak looks at each other, hold each other's gaze, but then she was ushered away by your grandmother.'

'So how did you meet her properly? How did you end up together?' asked Abby.

'Your grandmother gave up in the end. She said that there was something inevitable about us.'

His voice cracked a little and Abby moved towards him and slipped her hand into his.

'And then I started doing the puppets with them and the rest, as they say . . .'

'. . . is history,' added Abby.

They stood in silence for a moment before Dad bent and kissed her head.

'So,' asked Abby, 'what are we going to do?'

'I don't know,' he confessed.

Worry washed over Abby now. 'Dad, what if . . . what if we can't think of anything?'

Dad smiled down at her.

'I think that maybe Linda is right this time too . . .' he said. 'We need some positive thinking.' He squeezed her hand.

'We'll come up with something.'

After they'd finished at the pier, Abby walked Myra home. It was late on a Saturday and there was a general bustle on the promenade but, despite the warmth, Myra was quiet.

'You going to tell me what's wrong,' asked Abby, 'or do you want me to guess?'

Myra frowned and kept walking.

'Ok,' continued Abby, 'you stole your parents' credit card and bought a sports car on the internet without telling them, and want to take it for a spin?'

Myra rolled her eyes and shook her head. Abby frowned.

'How about, you found a unicorn living in your wardrobe and you can't tell anyone and he's keeping you up all night because you have to keep feeding him jam doughnuts every two hours?'

Myra was smiling now.

'Ok, last try. You want to tell me that you are, in fact, from the planet Zuzu and have been sent to Earth to live like a human female until you're thirteen, at which point you will resume your natural form and take over the world?'

Myra shook her head.

'Well,' sniffed Abby, 'I thought I was getting close with that last one.'

Myra poked her in her side. Abby waited for her to say something.

'I don't know—' Myra shrugged. 'I've been really down about the whole design thing. It's like I've hit a wall or something.'

'Er, did you even see the cloak you made?' asked Abby, flabbergasted.

Myra shrugged. 'That was simple, and anyway, Mum helped me.'

'But you're brilliant,' said Abby.

'That's what Mum said too.'

'Well she's right,' replied Abby.

'Er, news flash, your mum and your best friend are practically duty bound to tell you you're awesome. It's kind of the rules.'

'Well, that's not true. I would totally tell you if you were useless,' said Abby.

Myra raised her eyebrows at her. 'Really?'

Abby's eyes were troubled. 'Well, maybe I wouldn't say useless.'

'Ha, you see!'

'I wouldn't lie to you, Myra,' said Abby earnestly.

Myra's eyes softened and she linked her arm into Abby's as she usually did.

'I know. It's just that maybe I have to be realistic.'

'No,' said Abby stopping in her tracks, 'I don't think you have to be realistic at all. I hate that word. It's the most boring word in the world. It's about determination. About never giving up.'

Abby turned to face Myra now.

'What I've learnt over the last few weeks is that everyone sees the hour you're on stage. This small window when everything looks glitzy and perfect. They don't see the hours and hours of practice. The bumps and scrapes, the epic fails and the mishaps. The thing is,' confided Abby, 'that my dad is absolutely brilliant at failing.'

Myra let out a snort of laughter.

'I mean, he fails and fails. He is the definition of failure. He fails here, there and everywhere, and when you think he's found every possible way of failing, he finds some new ways.'

Myra was laughing now, and Abby loved to hear it. She hadn't heard her laugh like that for ages.

'I mean, if there was an Olympic medal for failure, he

would definitely get one. The thing is, every time he fails, he fails a little better, and I am starting to think that it is, in fact, his superpower.'

Abby held Myra's hands.

'Some kids get dads who are pilots, or who can swim the Channel. I get the king of fails!'

Myra's smile slowly faded.

'You can't give up, Myra. Not if this is what you want.'

'Maybe,' she said quietly.

'You know this new magic Dad and I have been doing? I can't tell you everything, not yet, but things are changing. I can feel it. It feels like anything is possible.'

Myra looked at her friend, 'I wish I could believe you.'

CHAPTER TWENTY

'D ad?'
    Abby woke up and he was nowhere to be seen. She looked at the balloon sausage dog he had made her last night, now looking slightly deflated by the bed, before walking over to Ta-da's enclosure, scooping him up and carrying him out to the shed.

'Dad!' she said as she walked into the darkness.

'Yup!?'

His voice was hard to pin down.

'Where are you?'

He popped up from behind some boxes like a startled rabbit.

'What are you doing?' she asked, smiling.

He started coughing from the dust.

'Looking for inspiration,' he mused. He looked just as

174

preoccupied as she had been for the last few days.

'I thought I might find something interesting back here, something that would give us an idea.'

'Annnd?' asked Abby, feeling Ta-da's furry warmth against her.

'Nothing. Nada. Zilch.'

He picked his way out of the jungle of stuff and clapped the dust off his hands. Then he stood, perplexed. 'You know what your mum used to say?'

Abby shrugged.

'Sometimes you can look too hard for something, sometimes you have to wait for whatever it is to find you.'

Abby took this in and smiled.

'I reckon a cup of tea and a rest might help,' he said. 'It might give us a bit of perspective.'

Dad made them some tea and they spent a quiet day pottering about. Abby played with Ta-da, hiding carrots all around his tunnels and timing how long he took to find them. Then they ate their lunch of corned beef sandwiches out on a blanket in the field. They loved to do that in the summer. No tourists would walk up here so they'd have the whole place to themselves. Dad sat wrinkling his nose against the sun. Abby had brought Ta-da and he was bouncing around in the long grass very excitedly indeed. Usually Dad would lie back and fall asleep after having lunch in the sun but he was feeling more reflective today.

'We need something bigger, better,' he mused. 'That was what astonished people back in the day, that the magic would become more and more magnificent. We need something that will wake up this town. Inspire them. Make them know that we see them, that we know them.'

He was reminiscing now, his eyes settling on the lost grandeur of the town below. 'It was such a lovely place for your mum and me to grow up, you know? When we were your age, we had the luxury of looking around at all the splendidness and thinking that anything was possible, but now everyone walks around with their heads down, it's like they have nothing to look up for. They're busy, busy. Busy doing not much really.'

Abby had lost sight of Ta-da, so she got up and walked around until she found him and steered his

Royal Bouncingness back towards Dad. Abby flopped down beside him.

'This is nice, though, isn't it?' he said.

Abby smiled at him, cuddling Ta-da to her belly and feeling the warmth of the sun on her face.

'Yes,' she answered. 'Yes it is.'

They sat in silence for a moment.

'So, have you given any thought to what you want for your birthday next week, Abby-cadabra . . . ? I know it's all go at the moment, but I haven't forgotten.'

When she was small, Abby used to count down the days to birthdays and Christmases but things had been a bit weird since Mum had died. It was like they had to find a new way of doing things, work out how to celebrate without her. That's why Dad always let her have cake in bed on her birthday and slowly, and over time, they had kind of gotten used to getting through them. Abby shook her head.

'You're getting more and more like your mum every day.'

Abby smiled.

Abby was getting taller, she knew that, and her body

was changing. When she was little, she missed her mum because she wanted to play with her, to hug her. Now Abby was changing into a woman, she would sometimes wonder what they'd talk about. What they'd agree on, whether they'd fall out like other teenage girls and their mothers. She felt Dad's arm around her.

'Well, let me know if you think of something, won't you?'

After supper on the bus, they made some more tea and Dad let the pigeons out so they could fly in the orangey-pink sky, their forms beautifully outlined against the blazing sunset. Abby sat on the bus steps and watched as they wheeled above them.

'Well, stick a tail on me and call me a donkey,' shouted Dad. 'That is it!'

Then, he ran towards Abby, pulled her out of the way and ran onto the bus. He ran to the table, skidded to a stop and grabbed a pen and paper, scribbling furiously. Abby followed him in, catching his excitement.

'What is it?' she asked, feeling her heart start to beat a little more quickly.

Abby watched as he sketched the stage, the auditorium, the balconies and then a structure on the stage . . .

'We'll need bright costumes for people to see us from the back, and we're going to need two volunteers, two children . . .'

He pointed to the middle balcony. Abby nodded, catching on. Then he slid the paper towards her . . . his eyes locked on hers.

'What do you think?'

Pins and needles shot through her body and she felt her hair stand on end. She couldn't speak, she just nodded.

'Yes?' he asked.

'Yes,' she answered, looking at the sun slip behind the vast sea behind them.

CHAPTER TWENTY-ONE

Beverley the care home manager had told Dad that he could use the recreation room as an HQ. The care home had been overwhelmed with donations since Abby and Dad's video had gone viral and since it was located very close to the pier it was perfect for carrying things back and forth. Beverley had got some painters in to smarten things up a little and had invested in a new TV and some plants, which made the place look a lot homelier. She'd also arranged for the residents to have weekly dance lessons for those who were mobile enough. Dad told Abby that Jamal was absolutely rocking it. When Abby walked in, she couldn't believe it. It was like the residents all looked ten years younger, as if the love they'd received from the community had invigorated them. There was a new energy about everyone, and the compliments and the support that the staff had received because of the video had made them really proud to work there. They'd been given pay rises, brought new uniforms and could even be caught whistling in corridors or organizing parties in the kitchen.

Dad had called a meeting and asked Abby, Myra, Linda, Jamal, Lenny, Glenys and Beryl to attend. Beryl never spoke much, but she was showing a lot more interest in the world around her so Glenys thought it would be nice for her to be invited too.

Linda placed the table out in the middle of the room and Dad distributed copies of the plan to everyone. Half the table had to find their glasses before they could inspect it.

'Jamal,' said Dad, 'you're an engineer.'

'Ah!' he answered. 'I used to be an engineer.'

'Nonsense,' replied Dad, 'once an engineer, always an engineer.'

Jamal's shoulders widened a little.

'We're going to need a structure on the stage like this.'

Jamal studied the sketch.

'Shouldn't be too much of a problem.'

'I've got plenty of old wood and paint in the shed,' said Dad.

Jamal instinctively gave him a salute, like he had always done when he worked in the Royal Navy.

'I know it's a lot, Myra, but we're going to need costumes, Abby too this time, so she doesn't look like a scruffy kid who's wandered off the street and onto the stage . . .'

'Thanks Dad.'

'You're welcome,' he smiled.

'How do you feel about that, Myra?' Dad asked.

Myra could feel everyone's eyes on her, and felt her face flush warm.

'Erm,' she said, quietly, 'actually . . .'

Everyone watched her expectantly.

'Erm, I think that . . .'

Myra cleared her throat now.

'I think I'm going to need some help,' she said, her voice growing louder, more confident.

'Absolutely,' said Dad, 'of course you will.'

'Ooh,' gasped Glenys as her hand shot up into the air. 'I'll help. I'd love to help.'

'Well, that's perfect,' answered Dad.

Myra smiled over at Glenys who winked back at her and mouthed, 'Stick with me, kid.'

Dad carried on delegating jobs. 'Linda will need to keep an eye on the spreadsheet.'

'I'm already doing that, Ronald,' she said, her arms crossed and rolling her eyes.

'And Lenny . . .' Dad continued.

Lenny was as usual engrossed in his phone. He didn't even look up.

'Lenny?' asked Dad again.

Linda sighed.

'OI, LENNY!' she shouted, making some of the older residents have to adjust their hearing aids.

Lenny looked up through his floppy fringe.

'You will be in charge of marketing.'

'What, me?' Lenny asked.

Dad's forehead creased.

'Are you called Lenny?'

'Uh-huh,' he answered shyly.

'Then you are in charge of marketing.'

'Cool.' And with that he went back to his phone.

Abby looked at him in wonder.

'What about me?' came a voice. Dad looked around to see a green-eyed woman smiling. She'd just come in and was carrying a pot of tea and a tray of small cakes. Abby had never seen her before yet there was something familiar about her. She had a walking stick and even though she was obviously old, there was something sprightly and youthful about her, with her long greying hair tied in a knot on her head.

'Well, everyone is welcome here,' he said. 'Please sit down.'

She walked towards the table and Abby felt she couldn't even look at her straight on. She sat down quickly.

'I'm Violet,' she said.

'Nice to meet you, Violet,' responded Dad. 'I don't think we've met.'

Violet nodded. 'I'm new around here. It would be lovely to make some friends,' she said. 'Is there any way I could help?'

There was something so engaging and warm about her face.

'Well, I don't know,' answered Dad. 'What do you do?'

'I am a cook,' she answered shyly. Dad's face brightened immediately.

'Well, Violet, you will be cakemaker-in-charge. Victoria sponges, scones, lemon drizzle. An army marches on its stomach. And everything in the world is better with cake.'

'Well,' she said smiling, 'that's splendid.'

Everyone looked content.

'The performance is in two weeks.' Everyone started talking at once and Dad put up his hand.

'I know, I know. Bit short notice, but I believe in us. We need to concentrate and get the job done, but we can do this.'

And then, they got to work. Glenys and Myra started sketching their ideas while Beryl was taken for a little rest. Abby turned around to see what Violet was doing but just as she had arrived, she disappeared once again.

CHAPTER TWENTY-TWO

'Stand still, will you?'

Abby was fidgeting as Myra was taking her measurements.

'I'm trying!'

Myra was kneeling, trying to get the measurement from Abby's ankles to her waist. She looked at the tape and read it while Glenys noted down the numbers. They'd already jotted down Dad's measurements and he was doing strongman poses for them and making them laugh but was secretly pleased as punch that the jogging, or lolloping, had started to pay off and he was feeling fitter and healthier and more energetic.

'I can't help it if I'm a dazzling example of the male species,' he said. 'I'm gourrrrgeous, absolutely gouuurrrrgeous.'

Myra giggled and Linda rolled her eyes. Dad started making tea for Jamal and Tony, who were starting on the wooden structure in the car park.

'Right, finished,' said Myra. 'You can go.'

Abby felt her shoulders relax. She had just about managed being in the limelight for the care home magic, but the thought of the new trick in such a large venue made her stomach turn over every time she thought about it. She'd woken up several times the night before, thinking about all the upturned faces, the dazzling lights and the possibility of things going wrong and had spent a good few tense hours listening to Dad snore before finally getting back to sleep.

'Er-hem.'

They all looked up. It was Lenny. He was holding a pile of paper. They looked at him in astonishment.

'Er, so. I . . . I made this poster. The image is like old-fashioned magic but mixed up with contemporary symbolism. It's digital art but I've done it in paper form so it's kind of a joke . . . I was going to put these up all over town and obviously do an online campaign.'

They looked at him, stunned. It was the most Abby

had heard him say in around two years. Dad put down the tray of tea and took the poster. It was beautiful. Old-fashioned in style but with an edge to it. The words 'The Great Ronaldo', and an image of Dad and Abby, looking like they came from the 1950s. Dad with slicked back hair and Abby looking glamorous.

'And then, I've got permission from the council to use this special spray paint to paint this symbol here . . .'

At this, he held up another piece of paper with a wand and two wings either side of it.

'It's a kind of visual tag of what you're doing. I want to spray them all over town like graffiti and then, because it's special paint, in a few weeks it'll fade like it was never there. So. Like magic . . .'

'That is so cool . . .' said Myra, her mouth agape.

'I have no idea what you just said, young lad,' said Glenys, 'but it's a very nice picture'.

Dad was beaming. He slapped Lenny on the back.

'You, my boy, are so incredibly talented.'

Lenny blushed a deep red.

'So creative!' he said. 'So clever!' Then, he pulled Lenny into a really awkward hug that lasted a little too long.

'Ok,' said Lenny extricating himself, 'I'm going to need some help putting all these up.'

'Abby?' asked Dad.

'I was thinking we should split up – you start at one end of the pier, and I'll start at the other and then, hopefully, we'll meet in the middle.'

Abby nodded. She looked at the poster in her hands.

'It's amazing, Lenny.'

Lenny shrugged. He was about to turn to walk to the north side of the promenade when he suddenly turned.

'Abby?' Lenny whispered.

Abby looked up at him. 'What?'

He looked uncomfortable now.

'My mum . . . Your dad . . . They've been spending a lot of time together recently . . . Mum doesn't stop talking about him.'

Abby frowned.

'And?'

'You don't think, well, you don't think they're, you know, together-together, do you?'

Abby's stomach flipped.

'No!' she retorted. His face relaxed.

'I mean, not that it's a problem, it would just be a bit weird . . .'

'No,' said Abby, 'I'm sure they're not . . . I mean, all they do is bicker, fight . . .'

'Like most married couples,' suggested Lenny.

Abby stood still a moment. Shook her head. 'No.'

He shrugged. 'Ok, I was just checking.' And then he turned and walked away, leaving Abby standing stock-still, her mind whirring.

*

Glenys went to her room to fetch a box of old patterns and notebooks and brought them back, putting them on the table in front of Myra.

'I held on to these in case they'd come in handy,' she said, smiling and starting to rummage through the box.

'What are they?'

'Pattern pieces, little reminders. Shortcuts. That kind of thing. I was a seamstress, and an old school tailor.'

Myra watched, wide-eyed, as Glenys started to spread the materials out onto the table. There were tailor's chalks and charts, pattern pieces and foam forms. A lifetime of sewing paraphernalia.

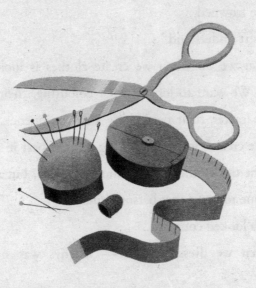

'I am so glad that you asked for help.' Glenys winked, smiling. 'Right then young lady, first things first . . .'

Glenys looked at her with a measuring tape around her neck.

'What is the purpose of creating something for someone to wear?'

Myra looked at her confused.

'What are we trying to achieve?' Glenys asked.

'We're trying to transform them, change them, I think . . .' Myra trailed off.

'Ah!' exclaimed Glenys. 'Rookie mistake. You are absolutely and perfectly wrong.'

Myra frowned.

'I don't understand.'

'What we do when we create clothes is look at a person. We want to look at their colouring, their eyes, their character, their personality, their uniqueness. And then, we create clothes that bring out the best in them. We want the clothes to be almost invisible, but at the same time to make that person shine.'

Myra looked confused.

'When we dress someone—' Glenys was smiling

at her gently now – 'we want them to be beautifully themselves . . . We don't want to see the clothes, really. We want them to be shining. The star attraction in their own show, because being yourself is the bravest thing you can do. You see lesser designers want to draw attention, to shout, but sometimes, all you need to do is whisper.'

Myra nodded. Then Glenys and her sat down and talked about Abby and Ron. About their characters and their stories. About Abby's shyness, about Ron's journey. And slowly and surely, they started sketching and changing and refining until they both stood back and thought they really had something special.

CHAPTER TWENTY-THREE

'Happy birthday to yooooou, Happy birthday to yoooooou, Happy birthday Abby-cadabra, Happy birthday to yoooooou.'

Abby opened her eyes to see Dad grinning and holding a chocolate cupcake with a candle on it. Ta-da was tucked under his arm.

'Come on then, blow it out.'

Abby smiled and pulled herself up and blew on the candle.

Dad pushed it towards her and said, 'Birthday breakfast of champions.'

He sat on the bed, Ta-da in his lap, watching.

'There's a few more where those came from too. Violet made them.'

Abby peeled off the paper and took a bite. It was delicious!

'Thanks, Dad.'

'There's a card here from Myra, and this . . .' he said, leaning over to his bunk bed and pulling a present out from under his bedcovers for Abby, 'is from me.'

Abby smiled.

'It isn't much.'

She pushed her fingers under the fold of paper and ripped it open.

'It's a photo album,' he said. 'I was thinking we could maybe make an album of our summer? Make some new memories. I think perhaps that after your mum died, we forgot we need new stories too. Lenny's got lots of photos we could stick on the front cover . . . What do you say?'

'Sounds perfect,' said Abby.

Dad ruffled her hair and kissed her head. Then he left Ta-da on the bed to go and put the kettle on.

Abby and Dad then spent the whole day practising. Dad had come up with some new tricks for the warm-up act. It was like he had the energy for new ideas again. He was making up more new illusions than he had done for years. He had one trick where he pulled glass after glass of water from his sleeve and lined them up on the table in front of him. Another, where using sleight of hand, he would ask someone to sign the back of a ten-pound note and then appear to rip it up into little pieces. He'd then ask another audience member for their wallet, and there it would be, put back together again, the signature intact. Abby was getting better at keeping her focus too – with practice she was finding it easier to slip into the spells and more confident in being able to keep them going for longer. They worked through the afternoon, only stopping for more cupcakes and tea when they heard Linda's voice. Dad looked at Abby in surprise. She came towards the shed . . .

'Oh, here you are, I've been phoning all afternoon!'

Dad explained that his phone was on the bus.

She was out of breath and hot.

'Happy birthday, Abby,' Linda said, coming over to give Abby a hot, sweaty hug.

'Thanks, Aunt Linda.'

'Sorry if I stink, I ran here.'

'It's alright.'

'Is that what you wanted?' asked Dad.

Linda rolled her eyes. 'I came to say happy birthday to

Abby here. Honestly, you aren't half-irritating, Ronald. I also wanted to say that the show has sold out.'

Dad looked at Abby.

'What do you mean it's sold out?'

'You can't get a ticket for love nor money . . . One thousand tickets sold, Ronald!'

They both looked at her in amazement.

'One thousand at twenty per cent of fifteen pounds a ticket . . .'

Dad did some quick calculations in his head.

'That's a lot of money!'

'Minus my cut, of course,' she reminded him.

'Of course.'

'They've been knocking at the door asking for more. They've had to close the box office and put signs up so people leave them alone.'

Dad sat down on a pile of old suitcases.

'This is amazing.'

'Well, let's not disappoint them. Are you two sure you can't add another night?'

Abby shot a look at Dad. He shook his head.

'No, it's a one-time thing. Like we said, we want to do

what the greats did, three shows in total.'

'Well, as your manager I'd ask you to reconsider. Can you imagine the money you'd make if you did a season of this? You'd be millionaires.'

'It's not possible,' answered Dad. 'Anyway, it's not why we're doing it. You've got to trust us on this one.'

Linda shrugged. 'Ok, well nothing you do has ever made any sense to me, Ronald, so I don't know why I was expecting this to be different,' she said. With that she turned and started to walk home.

Dad's shock started to soften a little. He looked over at Abby and smiled. 'This will be the biggest audience we've ever had. It's going to be phenomenal.'

Abby watched as Dad got up and did a little happy dance, trying not to panic at the thought of so many eyes watching them.

'Come on,' said Dad, pulling Abby to her feet. 'This is going to be splendid!'

CHAPTER TWENTY-FOUR

Myra had asked her parents to come over to the care home at six that evening. She arrived early to do some last-minute work on the costumes with Glenys, who had been teaching her about garment construction. They'd made mock-ups in a thin white cotton, and now they were working with the real material. Ron's suit was being made in a silver satin, so it would contrast with his magician's cape. Glenys was very impressed when Myra showed her the cape. They also covered his top hat in a deep indigo with silver stars to match his suit. Myra thought it would look good with his skin tone and capture that silliness and irreverence that Ron had. For Abby, they had gone with a top and trousers. The top was halfway finished but they hadn't even started the trousers yet.

As they worked, Glenys told Myra about her time as

a young seamstress in a theatre when she had just moved to London. How she'd made costumes for actors and singers, and how, when she was older, she had started her own business and made clothes and wedding dresses and christening gowns. Myra had listened rapt to Glenys's tales and Glenys started showing her all the tips and tricks and techniques that she had learnt over her fifty-year career. Myra was absorbing every instruction like a sponge, and Glenys was enjoying teaching someone who was so quick to learn. Myra felt herself grow in confidence with each cut, pin and stitch.

'You see,' Glenys explained kindly, as she watched Myra piece together the last elements of Abby's top, 'contrary to what most young people believe, talent is actually just the start. It has to be nurtured with practice, with knowledge, with skill.'

Myra was stitching the stars onto the top hat when she heard the unmistakable voices of her parents filling the reception area of the care home.

'It's Mum and Dad. They're here,' she said excitedly.

Myra stood up and waited for them, glancing over at Glenys. They came in looking a little bewildered,

Myra's mum smiling uncertainly.

'What's all the mystery about?' she asked.

Myra beamed. She looked at Glenys, who was trying to stay at a respectful distance.

'I've been designing . . . for a magic show. Making costumes . . .'

'What?' asked her mother, tilting her head.

'Abby and her dad are doing a show and Glenys and I, we've been making the costumes . . .'

Her mum looked over at their work.

'You're telling me that you have been making these?'

Myra nodded. Her mum approached the table and looked at the designs. Picked up Ron's jacket and studied the workmanship.

Myra shifted her weight from one foot to the other. Deepa said nothing. She took in every detail, held the garments up to the light. Myra looked over at Glenys nervously.

'So,' asked Myra, 'what do you think?'

Deepa turned now, her eyes glistening.

'I am so proud of you.'

Myra's shoulders seemed to broaden. She beamed at her mother.

'This workmanship is exceptional. The designs are flawless.'

'I . . .' began Myra, 'I asked Glenys to help me.'

Deepa smiled broadly at Myra.

'Well isn't that wonderful?' answered Deepa.

Deepa looked over at Glenys.

'I'm sorry, I don't think we've met, Mrs, er . . . ?'

'Call me Glenys, please,' said Glenys, coming over and putting out her hand, only to be enveloped in a hug by Myra's mum.

'The pattern-making is amazing,' said Deepa. 'Repairs and the basics I can do but you are so skilled.'

Glenys went all pink-cheeked and shy.

'I haven't said this in front of her before because I don't want her to get a big head,' said Glenys looking over at Myra, 'but I've taught a lot of people over the years and I have never seen someone so talented at such a young age.'

It was Myra's turn to feel her cheeks flush now.

'You are going to be a brilliant fashion designer,' said

her mum, turning to Myra once again. 'You have an eye for detail . . . colour . . .' Your father and I will find a way to send you to college, we'll sell the shop if we have to . . .'

Myra had tears streaming down her face by now.

'You'd sell the shop for me?'

'Of course we would,' replied her father. 'We built the business so we could support you in doing whatever you want!'

Myra started crying and pulled them both into a hug.

'So,' began Glenys, 'the reason we asked you here is that we thought we would get this all done in time, but . . .'

'When's the performance?' Deepa asked.

'Tomorrow night,' said Glenys. A shadow fell over Deepa's face.

'Well,' she said approaching the table, 'we better get cracking. Sanjeev! Get my sewing glasses from the shop and bring over my machine, we're going to need an extra one if we're going to get these costumes done.' Myra watched as her father ran out of the door, and her mum started to study the patterns they had cut with Glenys. Her eyes were full to bursting, but her heart was even fuller.

*

Abby and Dad drove down to the pier to see the finished set. When they arrived, Jamal and Tony were standing back admiring their handiwork. It was a smaller plinth in the middle of the big stage, so that the people on the balconies would be able to see better. They had painted the structure a dark blue and Tony had gone to town blobbing little white dots of paint all over it so it looked like the night sky. Dad slapped him on the back.

'It looks terrific, Tony. Absolutely terrific!' His voice carried around the pavilion.

Jamal and Tony stood there, leaning on each other's shoulders, looking very pleased with themselves indeed.

'I reckon it's time for chips all round,' said Dad.

He handed Abby a couple of ten-pound notes and winked at her. 'Remember to get an OAP discount on Jamal's chips, won't you?'

Abby smiled, then turned and walked out into the evening light. It was quieter now, the sandy-toed children who occupied the pier all afternoon having been packed into the back of cars. A few couples remained, lighting cheap barbecues on the beach. The magic show was tomorrow, and Abby just couldn't believe how quickly it had come around. Last night, she and Dad had looked through some old slides they needed for the trick. They'd dug out an old projector which flickered images and bits of film onto any white surface or wall. They'd hung up an old bed sheet on the washing line between the bus and the shed and projected pictures of Mum and Dad onto it. Then they'd drunk tea, both of them slightly lost in another world watching scratchy images from the past. The way Mum moved on stage though was mesmerizing. She was so good, so slick and so fast with her hands and tricks that she really did look magic. Abby felt her own stomach tightening while she watched her and thought how the show at the pier would go. She was sure that they could do it, but there were so many things that could go wrong, and she couldn't help but remember the disaster at the holiday park.

Suddenly Abby was jolted back to the present as her bag was yanked off her shoulder. She stared as the contents spilled out onto the pavement in front of her. She heard a laugh behind her.

'So you think you're some kind of celebrity or

something now, do you?'

It was Jasmine, her arms crossed. She walked past Abby. Ella was with her in denim shorts, a shirt tied around her waist. They were watching as she scrabbled to pick up her notebooks, pens and chewing gum. Thank goodness the magic book hadn't fallen out, but its corner was visible, shining in the twilight. Abby shoved it quickly back in and closed the bag, holding it protectively in front of her chest. It was enough to draw Jasmine's attention, and although she didn't say anything, Abby could feel her eyes on the bag.

'So how are you doing it?' Jasmine asked, sticking out her chin provocatively.

'Everyone knows your dad and you are complete losers, so how are you cheating?'

'We're not cheating,' Abby said, surprised by her own reply. They were really starting to get on her nerves.

'Something's going on, you don't go from zero to hero that fast without some funny business.'

'You know what, Jasmine, you really are boring you know?' Abby said.

Ella's eyebrows shot up in disbelief.

'This makes you feel good, does it? Walking about being obnoxious? Pushing Myra around? I know what you did to her.'

Jasmine looked like she'd just been slapped in the face by a wet flannel. Abby had had enough of the sniping and the cruelty. It all felt so stupidly pointless.

'Just go away and leave us alone, will you?' Abby could hardly believe her own voice, and it wasn't shaking either.

Jasmine looked stunned before pushing past her and shoving Abby with her shoulder. 'Watch your back, Abby-cadabra,' she smirked.

Abby turned to watch them as they walked away, trying really hard not to feel rattled by Jasmine's threat. She felt suddenly a little colder and grasped the strap of her bag a little tighter in her fingers. She waited for them to disappear before taking a deep breath and walking hastily towards the chip shop.

CHAPTER TWENTY-FIVE

The stage was set and the pier staff were getting the pavilion ready, sweeping floors and dusting and painting. The old place was coming back to life. The management had had to hire new ushers and, since there wasn't much work around in town, the queue of applicants had stretched halfway down the promenade.

Abby and Dad had driven down in the van, neither of them saying very much. Ta-da was a bit bouncier than usual and unable to settle. Abby had been awake most of the night, thinking about how many things could go wrong. Thinking about how many people would be watching them. Thinking about what Jasmine had said.

'Come on,' said Dad, and smiled at her. 'Let's do the get in, we'll feel better then.'

Abby smiled and, sure enough, going through the

motions they had done a million times was kind of soothing. They carried the props in past the staff who were all looking at them excitedly. Then they set everything up. Abby took the cage of pigeons and Ta-da with her to the green room, so they wouldn't be left alone on stage until the show started. Dad went to meet Linda, who wanted him to sign some paperwork in the box office, and Abby took a moment to soak in the atmosphere of the green room. It was really small, and Abby had noticed that weirdly, green rooms were very rarely actually green. They were usually painted in quite dull greys with peeling walls and unglamorous toilets. She let her eyes take in the long mirrors lined with lightbulbs and the makeup area. It was strange. She had been backstage so often over the years, on the side lines, but now she was here waiting to go on stage herself. She smiled as she remembered her mother putting on her bright makeup, brushing her hair. Abby imagined if she turned around now her mother would be standing there.

'The queue's started.' It was Linda.

Abby's shoulders tightened. 'Already?'

'Already. I've reserved seating in the front row for

Glenys, Jamal, Tony and everyone from the care home.'

Abby nodded.

'Least we could do, I thought.'

Abby smiled.

Linda looked at her. 'You're just like your mum, you know,' she said. 'You're getting more like her as time goes by.'

Abby looked back at the mirror.

'Even more beautiful, and an even bigger pain in my bum.'

Abby's smile broke into a giggle.

Linda watched her a moment. 'Are you ok with all this, though? It's a lot. You know, you don't have to do anything you don't want to . . .'

Abby nodded. 'I know, I'm just nervous, that's all.'

'Your mum would be too.'

Abby turned her gaze on her. 'Really?'

'Of course!' Linda said, as if that was obvious.

'She just seemed so together, so confident.'

'We're all a mixture of feelings, Abby, no-one is completely one thing or the other, even me . . . I'm not always absolutely sure I'm right about things—' she waved theatrically before placing her hand on her hip and reconsidering – 'though obviously I usually am . . .'

Abby rolled her eyes. Linda came towards the dressing table, checking out something that was stuck in her teeth in the mirror.

'Your mum could be stubborn, nervous, rude—' Linda lowered her voice conspiratorially – 'I even heard her swear once or twice . . .'

Abby smiled, felt the tears stinging her eyes.

'She was real, Abby. Flesh and blood, not this angel. And that didn't make her less of anything, it made her more blimmin' wonderful. It's important that you know that.'

Linda had removed whatever was in her teeth and was

checking out her outfit in the mirror now.

'No-one's perfect, Abby, your mum included. We fell out, and we fell in. And like the hokey-cokey, my lovely, that's what it's all about.'

There was a polite knock. Myra popped her head around the door, her mum behind her. 'Ready for costume?' Linda winked before heading out.

Abby nodded.

Abby hadn't actually seen her costume and Myra and her mum carried it inside a garment bag. Myra began to unzip it slowly and the colour flashed through into the grey room. Abby gasped when Myra pulled it out. It was breathtaking. It was made in an emerald green, with navy embroidery that was both beautiful and subtle. The top was long-sleeved with a soft cape in the back. The trousers matched perfectly, and had the same embroidery down each leg. Abby noticed that Myra was looking at her, worried . . .

'Oh! Myra,' she said, but she couldn't go further because everything she wanted to say wasn't enough. Myra smiled an enormous smile. Then she and her mum helped Abby get dressed. They pulled the top over her head. It fitted perfectly and the trousers were just the right length. They had found some plain shoes too, and had embroidered the letter 'A' onto each one. Myra's mum brushed Abby's hair as a finishing touch.

'I think you should leave your hair as it is, it's very beautiful,' said Myra's mum.

'I agree,' said Myra.

Abby stood in the mirror and really looked at herself for the first time in a very, very long time. She was changing. Even she could see that. She looked more grown up. The emerald green made her skin more luminous and her freckles stand out more. The navy contrasted with her hair, making it redder, deeper, more vivid. Myra came to stand beside her and smiled, 'You look amazing. You look just like you.'

Dad had also changed into his costume, a suit of deep navy and a waistcoat to match, both embroidered with silvery thread that looked like the Milky Way. He looked incredible. He gasped when he saw Abby, smearing a tear from his eye.

'You look beautiful,' he said. 'You ready?'

Abby nodded and they carried Ta-da and the pigeons

through the narrow maze of backstage corridors to the side of the stage. Dad had asked for the doors to stay closed until he gave the signal so that they could prepare.

'Everything's going to be alright,' whispered Dad. 'We know what we're doing.'

Abby almost couldn't speak. It was then that Dad nodded at one of the ushers at the door, and Abby and Dad went to stand in the wings, behind the black curtains. A whoosh of chatter came as the doors opened, and slowly and surely the auditorium filled. People trying to find their seats. Men, women and children alike. Abby's heart raced as she saw the front row being filled with Jamal, Beryl, Glenys, Violet and the care-home staff. There was a palpable excitement, an anticipation. Abby heard Linda behind her whisper, 'Good luck. Knock 'em dead,' and then everything fell into darkness as the house lights were dimmed. It was showtime.

'Ladies and gentlemen, please welcome the Great Ronaldo and Abby-cadabra!'

Abby's world exploded with light and the music Dad had chosen started playing. There was an almighty round of applause as they took the stage. They started with Ta-da and the box. It was a crowd-pleaser and brought gasps. Abby's nerves settled a little as she took Ta-da behind the structure on the stage. Then Dad did some close work and Abby crossed the stage and took a ten-pound note from a man in the front row, then asked the usher at the front to sign it. They did the trick brilliantly and everyone gasped when the ten pounds turned up in a lady's purse in the second row. Abby and Dad could sense that they were warming up nicely. Abby walked back on stage while Dad did the glasses from his sleeve trick. The audience clapped and laughed as he pulled glass after glass of water out of his sleeve: one, two, three, four, five, six, seven . . . The clapping came harder and harder, the laughter louder and louder. When he reached fifteen glasses, he did a comical kind of collapse in exhaustion on the floor. Jamal was laughing but Glenys looked a little concerned until Dad got up again, when she started clapping with delight along with everyone else.

Abby watched Dad. He was in his element, his new suit sparkling in the lights. He was performing in a way Abby had never seen before. With a new-found confidence that was spell-binding. He was relaxed. In control. In fact, he looked like a new man.

Before long, it was time for the pigeons. Abby had placed them under the table just before the show started. They had practised and practised, visions of what happened the last time they tried this trick haunting them both, but their calmness seemed to somehow soothe the birds too, and they were, thank goodness, cooperative. Dad took the empty box and threw it in the air and, lo and behold, it was full of pigeons. The audience were really leaning in now. Then Dad tossed it again and they were gone. Gasps abounded and then he asked everyone to look up, and there they were flying around in circles overhead. The whoops were deafening. And then, just like that, the lights went up and it was time for the interval. Abby and Dad had planned it like this so they had enough time to catch the pigeons again and calm them down before the real magic in the second half. The children all started to queue for ice-cream and Dad and Abby waited off stage.

Linda brought them some water. She nodded at them. 'It's brilliant.'

Dad was smiling but there was an edge to him. A

heightened state of being. Abby felt sick, it was almost time for the main magic, but thinking about the fact that her mum also used to get nervous, made it easier somehow. Linda looked at her watch. Five minutes. By the time the lights went down again, Abby felt like she was actually going to heave. Dad held her hand and whispered, 'Enjoy it,' and then they stepped on stage once again. The lights were more subdued this time.

Dad began by telling a story. 'In this town, many years ago, there was a boy, and a girl. And even though they were young, they loved each other very much.'

A projector showed old photographs of Mum and Dad as children, holding hands and eating ice-creams.

'They had everything they ever wanted, and the girl and the boy grew up together and got married and they believed anything was possible.'

Abby felt a lump in her throat.

'They believed that they could be anyone, or anything. They believed that nothing could hold them back, that nothing could stand in their way, but one day the girl was gone, and the boy thought that he would never be happy again.'

There was a deadly silence now. Abby choked back tears.

It was at this point that Dad had asked an usher to find a young girl and a young boy from the balcony and bring them on stage. Abby watched as the usher led the chosen girl and boy down the steps and into the spotlight.

'But she had left him three things. Three gifts. A daughter who he was so proud of . . .'

Abby felt her cheeks burning.

'. . . and a hope that magic will always come again . . .'

Everyone was listening now.

'. . . and a belief that no matter how small you are, no matter how difficult your life, you will always rise.'

This was Abby's cue. She slipped behind the structure where she could be unseen while Dad pulled some sweets from behind the young children's ears and made them laugh. The audience clapped and then Abby opened the book.

'Shall we go back to your seats?' Dad asked the kids.

An usher moved towards the stage but Dad put his hand up and took the children by the hands, one either side of him.

Abby was already concentrating on a flying spell from the silver middle section of the book, her heart racing. And then, much to her relief, the ink started to move, to lose its shape and find another form. It was glistening. Finding itself. Moving towards itself. She studied. Concentrated. Tried to shut everything out and turned to glance quickly.

'Infantio . . . levata . . . infantio . . . levera . . .'

And then, Dad and the children's feet were lifting . . . and suddenly, the audience gasped. Abby couldn't hear anything. Not a pin-drop. She recited the words harder, faster and as she did, her dad and the children moved off the stage, their feet hanging in mid-air. Dad looked at them comfortingly. They smiled back at him, and the little girl squealed excitedly. And they floated, upwards, upwards towards the balcony where their parents had gotten to their feet in complete awe.

Everyone was rising to their feet now as Dad and the children hovered fifty feet in the air. Dad looking to all the world like he was just popping them back to their seats in the most normal fashion ever. They moved closer and closer to the balcony and then he casually took them over to their parents who stood, mouths agape. Then, he doffed his top hat politely, placed it back on his head and made his way back to the stage. They all watched him go, his cape glimmering mysteriously in the light. It was still incredibly quiet, save for the odd gasp and one person fainting, but, as his first foot touched the stage there came an instantaneous burst of applause and shouting, the loudest that Abby had ever heard. People were overawed, they were dumbfounded, they were crying. They were laughing. Abby watched as the ink on the spell disappeared. They had shared it alright, in the most incredible fashion, and now, it was gone.

Abby put the book back in her bag and made her way to the stage. They stood for a second, taking in the clapping, and then Dad pointed his magic wand theatrically towards the central chandelier above the stage as they'd rehearsed and the lights went out, leaving the audience in absolute darkness.

Dad and Abby had to be shown through the back entrance to the van because there was a commotion in the foyer and along the promenade. People just didn't want to leave. They were hanging around, waiting for an explanation. Abby and Dad said they'd meet the gang back at the care home and placed the pigeons and Ta-da in the van before jumping in themselves. They sat there in silence.

'Well, that went alright,' smiled Abby.

'It wasn't too bad, was it?'

And then they screamed. Shouted. Laughed until they had tears flowing down their faces.

'Come on,' said Dad, 'let's go see everyone.'

Beverley and Violet had organized a little party. There were balloons and music and Beryl was even tapping her foot to the tunes. Jamal was explaining to Lenny what he had done in the Navy. Myra's mum and dad were dancing, and Glenys and Linda were going over the night beat by beat. When Abby and Dad walked in, they all cheered and hugged and Abby couldn't believe how they had all managed it. Then they ate, all together, all chatting and laughing and Beverley even went to get some fizzy wine for the adults that she'd been saving for a special occasion. After that, they all kicked off their shoes and danced. Abby with Myra, Jamal with Glenys and Linda with Dad. Abby watched them a moment. She couldn't stop Lenny's words from buzzing in her ear but she still couldn't believe it either.

It was then that Myra nudged her. There was someone at the back door to the car park. It was Josh. Abby shrugged and they walked over to him.

'I just wanted to say it was brilliant.'

Myra looked at Abby.

'Thanks.'

Josh nodded and turned to go. Myra thought he looked a bit lost.

'You want to come in?' asked Myra. 'I mean, there's plenty of food, lemonade, dandelion and burdock, whatever that is. I think it might be something that old people used to drink back in the day.'

Josh smiled. 'Thanks,' he said, 'that'd be great.'

Myra turned and Josh followed her to the table, and Abby looked back at Dad and Linda dancing and laughing, having the time of their lives.

CHAPTER TWENTY-SIX

A bby opened her eyes, the early morning light coming through the curtains. Something was different. She could hear her dad still snoring, but there was another sound. Linda had come back after the party to drink hot chocolate and laugh but it wasn't her on the sofa either. It was like a low hum, or a deep buzzing. She put her hand up against the wall of the bus and realized that the window was vibrating. She shot upright and opened the curtains and there, above the bus, was a helicopter. Abby squinted as it descended, agitating the long grass in the field. On its side was emblazoned, 'ECHO NEWS'. Abby blinked, unsure whether she was awake or dreaming. Then, as it touched down, the door slid open and a man with a microphone jumped out.

'Err, Dad,' she said. 'DAD!'

Dad had only just pulled
on his trousers when there
was a knock on the bus
door.

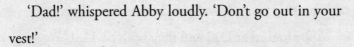

'Good morning!
It's Terrel Richardson
from Echo News.
Can we have a word,
please?'

'Dad!' whispered Abby loudly. 'Don't go out in your
vest!'

Dad grabbed a shirt and buttoned it up wrongly, but
at least he was decent, and then Abby and Linda dressed
quickly and watched as Dad did an interview with the
biggest news station in the world in the field, his hair
sticking up and his shirt done up all wrong.

Afterwards, Dad's phone started ringing on the table,
one call after another, and Abby and Linda knew that
something big was going on.

The performance had been a sensation. A wonder.
Lenny had filmed it and edited the video and circulated
it. It had outdone the first video and everyone wanted

to speak to them. Cars started arriving in the field and journalists in spiky heels from posh papers came staggering through the undergrowth. There were local rags and national newspapers and everything in between. Linda grabbed Dad and shut the bus doors. Then she went around closing all of the curtains.

'What do we do?' asked Dad.

Linda started thinking.

'Umm, we have to be really careful who we talk to . . . are you sure you just want to do one more show?'

Abby looked at Dad and they both nodded.

'So, we've got to hold out for the best offer.' That kind of made sense.

'So,' she said thinking on our feet, 'let's use the media to help us get our message out there . . .'

'The message being?' asked Dad.

'That there'll be one more show, Ronald,' said Linda, exasperated, 'and that you'll be fielding offers . . .'

'Ok,' nodded Dad, mentally preparing himself.

'Well, go on then . . .'

Dad was about to move when Linda interrupted him.

'No, not you. Abby.'

'Me?' asked Abby.

Linda nodded.

'You're half of this and it'll sound better coming from you.'

'She's right, it'll seem more mysterious . . .'

'Plus they've already seen your ugly face . . .'

'Thanks, Linda.'

'What, you want me to go now?'

'Well, after you've brushed your hair obviously, Abby, you look like something the cat fur-balled up.'

'Thanks, Aunty Linda.'

Abby nodded.

'Ok, it's the last show.'

'The last show.'

Linda made Abby change her T-shirt because it had ketchup on it and waited for her to put on her shoes.

'You ready?' asked Dad, his hand on her shoulder. Abby looked up at him, nodded and opened the door. She stepped down and the flashlights started along with the furious clicking of cameras. There must have been fifty there by now. They were all shoving microphones in her face.

'We're going to do one more show,' said Abby, trying to keep the shakiness out of her voice. 'It'll be the biggest and the best.'

There came another wave of camera clicks.

'Make us an offer and we'll come to your town and you will see real magic. No tricks, no illusions, real magic.'

At this the journalists bristled with excitement.

'Where do you wanna go, love?'

'How much does it cost, eh?'

'What's your name, darling?'

The questions came thick and fast, but Linda was there to fish her out of the throng and pull her up the stairs to safety.

Abby was breathing heavily. 'What do we do now?' she asked.

'We wait,' answered Linda, 'hold our nerve, don't take the first offer we get.'

There was about a two-minute silence until the phone started ringing.

Dad and Abby were stuck on the bus all day while Linda negotiated. Abby and Ta-da would peek at the journalists and newscasters, all sitting on bits of wood and the old chairs in their steel-grey suits, looking like a flock of jackdaws which had landed in the wrong habitat. Linda felt sorry for them in the end and started making trays of tea to take outside between phone calls. Abby and Dad also ate lunch in tense silence and watched as Linda seemed to get more and more steely. She was like a champion poker player. There would be no emotion on her face at all. Abby had no idea how Linda was able to contain it like that, because, like her dad had always said, anything you would want to know about Abby could be seen in her eyes, her face. She just couldn't hide it.

'Ah-ha, uh-huh. No thanks, we're looking for considerably more . . .'

She put the phone down for what felt like the hundredth time that day.

'What if we never get an offer good enough?' asked Dad, doubt starting to creep in.

Linda looked at him sharply.

'What I have learnt over the years, Ronald, is that you must never underestimate your own worth. There will be plenty of people in the world who will do that for you, so do not do it to yourself.'

After that it went quiet. Deathly quiet. Dad had started pacing the length of the bus and Abby had made the fiftieth cup of tea for herself that day. And then the phone rang. Linda answered. Her voice even.

'That sounds a bit more like it. M-hm. Yes, sir.'

Dad raised his eyebrows at Abby and mouthed 'sir'?

'Yes. We understand. A week's time? M-hm. Well, it's nice to do business with you too . . .'

And then she finished the call, put the handset down on the table and promptly fainted.

'Linda? Linda!'

Dad and Abby got her back on her feet and Dad slapped her cheeks to bring her round. Abby ran to the sink to get her a glass of water and watched as Dad held it to her mouth until her eyes started getting a little less fuzzy.

'You ok, Linda?'

'I'm fine,' she said. 'I'm fine.'

'So?' asked Dad.

Linda looked at him.

'It was the Mayor of London.'

'The Mayor of London?'

Linda nodded.

'A big show. A week today, for the end of summer.'

'Yes . . . ?' replied Dad.

'One performance . . . on TV. Right Now TV want to broadcast it live to the country and to the world.'

'Ok,' Dad replied, his eyebrows raised.

'They're offering a fruit basket—'

'Forget about the fruit basket, Linda, we can buy our own bananas—'

'—And a million pounds.'

'A MILLION POUNDS?' asked Dad. Linda nodded. It was Dad's turn to faint. Abby watched open-mouthed as he dropped to the floor. Linda got up and casually stepped over him.

'Well, while you're processing things, Ronald, I guess I'd better go tell the paparazzi . . .'

CHAPTER TWENTY-SEVEN

Summer was reaching its peak and since the night at the pier, new tourists were flocking to the town. It was like the magic of that night was still there somehow. The pier management had even decided to reopen the auditorium and had put out an open call for singers, dancers and local talents. There was a new buzz about the place. People smiled at each other. There was a new sense of energy and optimism. Whenever Dad or Abby walked around the town, people would stop or wave or shout something nice.

They only had a week. The Mayor of London wanted some magic to lift the city's hearts before summer came to an end, and Dad and Abby had been racking their brains ever since. Dad had actually been in shock for about three days. Rubbing his head and ringing Linda every couple of hours to make sure she hadn't been pulling his leg, but she reassured him that she wasn't.

'We've got one last trick and we have to make it bigger, better, more meaningful.' Dad rubbed his face. He hadn't shaved since the phone call from London and he smelled slightly of sweat and desperation.

They could go wherever they liked in London. They'd get any help they needed. The Right Now TV station were paying for most of it, and wanted to film it all. Jamal, Lenny, Tony, Myra and her parents and Glenys were all awaiting instructions. All they had to do was tell them how to prepare and they'd do it. They were a well-oiled machine by now, all champing at the bit. This was their opportunity to leave their mark.

The first thing Dad had done once he'd come round was to go to the bookshop in town and buy a map of London. When he returned to the bus, he spread it out on the table. They then sat in stunned silence drinking tea and eating bacon sandwiches and thinking about what on earth they were going to do. Abby picked up Ta-da and held him as she watched Dad wrestle with different ideas. They had one kind of spell left. A disappearing spell. Their last one. And they had to come up with an idea of how to use it in a way that would amaze however many people would come and see it, and others who would watch it on TV.

Dad had sketched idea after idea before ripping the paper from the notebook and throwing it on the floor. Then, they'd gone through Abby's books about the greatest magicians, seeing if that would spark anything, but to no avail. Dad was looking worried now, his eyes sunken. They only had four days left and he'd had to turn off his phone because Linda was calling him every half hour, wanting to know what was going on.

'You know, I heard someone say we should enjoy this . . .' said Abby, smiling softly.

Dad looked at her steadily.

'You know what? You're absolutely right,' replied Dad. 'We'll figure something out. It's just that so few people get this kind of an opportunity. These are the kinds of moments that you look back on when life passes you by and think wow; and I mean, it's a million pounds.'

'I know,' replied Abby.

'A million pounds,' he said again.

'I know,' she repeated.

They sat in an uncomfortable silence for a moment.

'I don't . . . I mean . . . I don't think we need it all,' Abby said.

Dad's shoulders relaxed and he laughed.

'Thank goodness for that,' he said. 'That's my girl. I've been thinking the same thing!'

'I mean,' mused Abby, 'the town library could do with some.'

'And the pavilion, I was thinking.'

'Maybe we could help Myra and Lenny with college too?'

Then, they talked themselves into a comfortable silence, the money not weighing on either of them anymore.

'We'll just keep as much as we need for a rainy day, and maybe an adventure or two,' smiled Dad. Then, he got up and went to take a shower.

Abby got up to put Ta-da back in his tunnels and walked outside. It was getting late, and the harsh light of early summer had mellowed into the golden smudginess of its end. The sky was pastel pink. She walked out into the long grass, kicking up moths as she went and sat down overlooking the town. It looked perfect. The sun warming the old place. The pier wandering off into the sea. Abby sat thinking about the show on the pier. The way the air had sparkled with electricity somehow. The way everyone in that room opened their hearts. She listened as the summer bees hummed lazily around her. Then she thought about how everyone had wanted to escape their everyday lives. The busyness, the endless stream of things to do. The way they wanted to get lost in the magic. When they were watching a show, all that existed was the present; tomorrow and yesterday just didn't exist. And then an idea started to form, her mind started working. Her heart started to beat a little faster. Would it even be possible? She got up and stood for a moment overlooking the town, the warm breeze in her hair, feeling a little older, a little wiser, and then she ran onto the bus and while Dad was still showering she started sketching the biggest trick she could have dreamed of. One that might not even be possible, but that if they pulled it off would be talked about for years. She sketched and sketched until she was finished, and

then Dad came to look over her shoulder. His hair was still damp and a towel hung around his neck. He studied the drawing, then picked up the paper and Abby was sure she saw his hands start to shake.

CHAPTER TWENTY-EIGHT

'Right,' said Linda, slapping a big folder of paper on the table in the sewing room. Everyone had been asked to get to the care home early. Jamal was drinking coffee and Beryl had been wheeled in to listen. Glenys was there, little pink curlers poking out of the scarf on her head. Myra and her mum and dad had come over before opening the shop and Beverley and Violet were passing around mugs of tea and toast thickly spread with butter. Lenny was yawning, his hair an absolute disaster, his teenage brain not used to getting up at this hour. Linda gave him a death stare before carrying on.

'We need Jamal to make a plan for a scaffold.'

Jamal saluted silently.

'The magic will take place outside. There will be no tickets. No fee to come and watch. The TV company and the Mayor of London are paying for the show so that anyone, money or not, can come. There'll be screens in lots of towns and cities too, including the pier pavilion here for anyone who can't travel.'

There was a rumble of approval at this.

'The scaffold will be put up by a team the mayor will organize, we just need the plan. And it will be put up on Parliament Square.'

Glenys put her cup of tea down at this. 'Goodness me.'

'Lenny,' Linda continued, 'we'll need a new poster. The TV company got in touch and they want to use your artwork.'

Lenny raked back his fringe with his fingers at this and almost fell off his chair.

'I know I am chairing this meeting and dislike any soppy emotion, but I'm very proud of you, boy. This will get you lots of opportunities. You'll need to make the most of them. You're a nice boy. You've got your head on straight and I love you.'

Her deadpan delivery couldn't even dampen the shock that Lenny felt and Abby was sure that there were tears in his eyes.

'Right, enough of that. Costume wise, we need bright. Ron and Abby are going to be up above the crowd. They need to be seen. There will be a camera on them that will project to a bigger screen so that more people can see too.'

Myra and her parents nodded.

'They won't be moving much, so anything goes. There are no budgetary constraints.'

At this, Sanjeev stopped eating his toast.

'No budget limit?' he asked.

'Have whatever you want to make the costumes.'

'And, it will be on TV?' asked Glenys excitedly.

'Yes,' said Linda.

'That's incredible. We'll have to ask them to put it on in the day room,' she said.

'What do you mean watch it in the day room?' asked Linda, slightly abruptly.

Glenda looked around embarrassed, 'Well, on the TV.'

'Nonsense,' said Linda, 'you won't be watching it on TV. You will be there.'

'Me?' asked Glenys.

'All of us,' said Linda smiling.

'We're ALL part of this. One for all. I'm organizing a bus. Beryl, Violet, Glenys, Jamal. All the care staff. Every bloomin' one of us.'

Dad smiled and winked at Abby. 'No-one will be left behind, got it?'

Glenys nodded.

'Right then,' Linda concluded, slamming the file back down on the table, 'we've got three days. Let's get our skates on.'

Jamal and Dad went to start sketching straight away so they could send the plans to London. Lenny went home to work on his next poster. He left as if he was walking on air. Then Abby sat with Myra and her parents as they started on ideas for the costumes.

'Red?' suggested Myra. 'They'll be far away, like they're two flames, lighting up the sky.'

'With gold for Abby,' added Myra's mum, 'a warm gold to light up her hair.'

Abby watched as they worked, each one finishing the

other's sentences. Myra doing the design, Glenys and her parents keeping an eye on technique.

Then Josh turned up to help. He knocked at the back door, looking shy, but proceeded to help with the beginnings of the pattern-making.

They worked all day until the scaffold design was done and sent to London. Dad felt proud that he could go and buy fish and chips for everyone, and they all sat around eating and talking about what it would be like to be in London.

'A-hem.' Dad was on his feet now.

'I just wanted to say—' he looked around – 'that these last weeks have been magical for many reasons.'

Abby looked over at Myra who was sitting with her parents.

'It's no secret that Abby and I, we lost our belief in magic for a little while, but I think we were looking for it in the wrong places. I think it had been all around us all along.'

Abby watched as Glenys wiped away a tear, and Myra's mum smiled at her dad.

Dad cleared his throat. 'We had turned inwards,

forgotten how to open up. You all know this will be out last show. I wanted to thank you for your love and support and your enthusiasm.'

Jamal saluted as usual and said, 'I'd like to say something too.'

Jamal was a man of few words, so when he did speak, everyone listened. 'I just wanted to say thank you for including us,' he said looking around at Beryl and Glenys and everyone else. 'I think I can speak for all of us in saying that we haven't had this much fun in years!'

Everyone cheered this time.

'I think you've made us see that we still have something to give. That there's a lot of life and mischief in us yet!'

Dad was nodding, tears in his eyes. 'Abso-blimmin-lutely!' he said. 'We are quite the team, so let's make this last trick truly spectacular!' There came another raucous cheer and Dad squidged Abby to him and kissed her head.

Afterwards, everyone got back to work until it was late. Abby folded away some material and watched as Josh helped Myra pack up the sewing machine and carry it back to the laundry room. Then she felt a presence by her side. It was Glenys, winding a bobbin with thread. Glenys followed Abby's gaze. Abby smiled vaguely, and watched as Myra and Josh tried to come out of the sewing room door at the same time, jamming and bumping into each other. They both laughed and Josh looked up to find Abby's gaze on him, so he smiled and gave her a shy little wave.

'It can be a little tricky when two friends become three,' Glenys ventured. Abby looked back at her and smiled. 'Oh, it's not that,' she answered.

Glenys's face softened, 'What is it then?'

'I don't know.' Something had been bugging her about Josh, but she just couldn't find the words for it. 'I suppose it's just that Josh didn't want anything to do with us, until we started becoming well-known. He used to be friends with some girls who gave us a really hard time and now, he's here helping out. Don't you think that that's a bit . . . I don't know . . . suspicious?'

Glenys put the bobbin in a box with the others.

'The dangers of fair-weather friends, you mean?'

'Something like that, I suppose . . .'

Glenys was watching Myra and Josh too.

'Well,' she replied, 'I've been in the world long enough to know that people change . . . or they grow braver. Time will tell . . . sometimes you have to give someone the benefit of the doubt. Give them enough time and they'll show you who they are . . .'

CHAPTER TWENTY-NINE

A bby and Dad slept in after working late. The phone was ringing and ringing but they ignored it. Linda had given them a folio of all the papers they had been featured in. It seemed that everyone in the world wanted to know how they were doing it. How they had made two little children fly. How they had made an old lady look and feel as if she was young again. Abby had been looking through the clippings as she drank a mug of tea. It seemed that everyone was ready for the impossible, that there was an appetite for change.

The phone rang again and Dad looked at it and sighed, quite exhausted.

'Fancy taking the birds for a flight?'

Dad put the pigeons in the basket and Abby fished out the old tandem and squashed her helmet onto her head.

Then they cycled the whole way to the top of the hill and took the book to the woods so they could practise the disappearing spell once again. Abby disappeared Dad and then a bush and then a tree. They laughed and played and sat for sandwiches and squash.

'What does it feel like?' asked Abby eventually.

'When you're disappeared?' Dad was uncapping his squash bottle.

'It's like you're free,' he said, 'it's like you're weightless, formless.'

Abby nodded her head.

'It's really peaceful,' he said again.

'Speaking of which . . .' said Dad and he got up and brushed himself off. The pigeons were getting a bit irritated now.

'Three! Two! One!' Abby and Dad said together and WHOOSH! Off they flew.

Dad laughed as they ran through the woods and out towards the tandem, where he jumped almost wholly over the fence and onto the bike. Abby followed him, laughing and breathless, until she was sitting on the back, pedalling with all her might and racing the pigeons home.

That night after supper, Abby watched as the moths bumped their heads on the bus window, trying to get to the lamps inside, and made her way slowly to bed. She lay there, listening to Dad washing up and brushing his teeth and eventually making his way to his own bed and turning off the light. She slid her hand down and felt the side of the book with her fingers and waited for sleep to come. It didn't, of course, even though she was exhausted as she started to think of London, of the crowds. Linda had said there could be thousands. Thousands and thousands. There would be no limit as they were outside. Her stomach started to tighten as she thought about this. Then, eventually, she got up once again and sat, her legs dangling off the edge of the bed, looking through a gap in the curtains towards the shed. She slid onto the floor, and walked down the aisle of the bus. It was dark now as she pushed the bus doors open and grabbed a lamp to take outside with her.

She stepped barefoot onto the ground outside the bus and felt the coolness of the night air wrap itself around her. She walked in her nightie towards the shed, the lamp casting a comforting glow around her. She looked at the dark shapes in the shed and the shadows and listened to the soft wing scrapes of the pigeons in their loft.

She went to find Grandma's trunk and knelt before it. She let her fingers run over the travel stickers in the soft glow of the light. Their colours seemed more vivid somehow, more alive. Then she opened it. Looked at the familiar red dresses. The dancing shoes. The puppets. She found herself with tears falling down her face. She didn't even know where they had come from, but they were there. She pulled out one of her mother's dresses. One she remembered her mum performing in. It was red too. She held it to her face a moment.

'Abby?' It was her dad. Barefoot. His hair sticking up. He came over and knelt beside her.

'What if I can't do it?' she asked, still holding her mother's dress. 'What if I'm not good enough? I'm never going to be as good as Mum.'

Dad's face fell. 'Is that what's worrying you?' he asked

gently. He reached out and rubbed her tears from her cheeks.

'I can't remember enough of her to be like her.'

'Oh, Abby,' he said, and squished her to him.

'I miss her,' she said. Abby pulled away, her face hot with tears.

'When your mother died, I thought we had lost her, but what all this has done is to make me realize that she was here all along. With us. She inhabits you, she inhabits us, she is all around us in the people that love us. But you are your own person, Abby. You are you. You are so wonderfully you! That is all your mother and I ever wanted for you. For you to take the stage in your own life, to be totally and utterly yourself. You get to choose, but whatever you do, own it, be it. Put your whole beautiful heart into it.'

Abby looked at him through the flickering lamplight.

'Do . . . Do you think she sent us the book?' asked Abby quietly.

'I don't know,' said Dad. 'But I'd like to think so. Maybe she knew we needed it?'

Abby nodded, tears streaming down her face now.

'I think she wanted to remind us that although life can take things away from us, it can give us great gifts too,' he said into her hair. 'Don't waste your precious life watching from the wings.'

Abby nodded, her voice failing her.

Then they hugged. They hugged and hugged and stayed there for a long time, the lamp casting magical shadows all around them.

CHAPTER THIRTY

Flasks of tea and sandwiches had been piled into baskets and carried onto the coach. Violet had made some Victoria sponges and drizzle cakes, and they had been carefully wrapped in greaseproof paper and taken aboard. The coach they'd hired was parked behind the care home and Beverley had made sure that everyone had gotten up early and had a slap-up breakfast. They'd started an hour earlier to get everyone on the coach because some of the residents were a bit slow-moving. It was going to be a long day, so they were getting everyone on one by one, and Tony, who had volunteered to drive the coach, had made sure that there were plenty of books and blankets and things on board to keep everyone happy.

Abby and Dad were travelling down in the van which

was parked outside next to the coach so they could journey to London in a kind of convoy. The van first and the coach behind it. Everything of theirs was packed and ready in the back of the van including the book in Abby's bag and Ta-da in a travelling pod. Linda was barking orders at everyone from the care home doorway, a pencil behind each ear and an eighties shoulder-padded power jacket that she'd found somewhere at home. Lenny was going to travel on the coach too and Josh had turned up to help out.

'I think that's perfect,' said Myra. Abby couldn't see herself. In the recreation room, they were having a last-minute fitting of the costumes that Myra and her parents and Glenys had miraculously turned around in three days. Myra checked the length of the dress on Abby and kneeled on the floor beside her.

'Yes, it's fine,' she said. Myra looked back at her mum, who beamed at her.

'It's beautiful, Myra.'

Abby's dress was a deep tomato red that made her hair shine. It was encrusted with gold embroidery and the most beautiful beading. At the back was a cape, that was attached at the shoulders and swept the floor. It was both light and substantial and glistened even under the care-home lights.

Myra got up. 'I wanted you to know that I embroidered your mother's initials into the design.'

Abby looked down and, sure enough, even though she hadn't seen it, her mother's initials were there, in every cluster of embroidery. Hidden but luminous. Intangible but present. Abby felt the tears spring to her eyes. Myra smiled.

'I thought it was important that she was with you tonight.'

Abby tried to speak but she just hugged Myra to her. Myra's mum dabbed the tears from her eyes.

'Right,' said Myra eventually, 'get it off so we can pack it up for the journey and put it on the coach.'

Abby went to the laundry room and changed out of the dress and gave it to Myra's mum, who was going to go down on the coach with the costumes. Myra, Sanjeev and Josh were going to help organize the screening in the pier pavilion and join everyone down in London later on.

'Good luck.' It was Violet. She'd appeared from

somewhere with her sparkling green eyes. She smiled at Abby. She was wearing a beautiful pillbox hat, also green, and a fitted suit that seemed timeless, her handbag clutched against her.

'Thanks,' said Abby smiling.

'You'll be splendid!' she said, and walked out towards the coach.

'Right,' barked Linda to an almost empty room, 'we've only got Beryl left to get on. Give me a hand, will you?'

Abby nodded, and while Dad helped Tony put the costumes in the coach's hold, Abby and Linda helped Beryl onto the coach. They wheeled her in her chair towards the steps, and just as they helped her get up, she slipped a little and needed to take a break.

'It's ok,' said Linda kindly, 'take your time.'

Eventually, she got moving again and smiled at them when they managed to get her into her seat.

The coach door closed, with Linda on board to take care of things. There were only Myra and Sanjeev left now to lock up, and Josh who stood waving. In the commotion of helping Beryl into the coach, they hadn't seen Jasmine and Ella turn up outside the open van door, rummage in Abby's bag and take the book, laughing to themselves.

CHAPTER THIRTY-ONE

Abby and Dad drove down to London in what felt like complete silence. Abby would look back occasionally and see the coach trundling down the road behind them. They had been given orders as to where to park and some passes to show any police that stopped them, since there would be a no-drive zone around Parliament Square for the show.

The old van growled as she tried to pick up a bit of speed, because even though she'd had a paint job, she was still the same old rickety van underneath it all. Every time Abby thought about the magic, her stomach would lurch.

Abby had never been to London. She'd seen pictures, of course, and they had done work on London in school, but being here felt like another thing entirely. As they drove into the city, it was like they were arriving on a film set. Everything looked so familiar because she had seen it on TV, but she still laughed at the red buses and the black cabs and how busy and important everyone looked. They stopped at some lights and flocks of bikes flew past like birds. And there was so much noise!

Dad didn't quite know where he was going and they had a few scary moments on roundabouts, but eventually they saw the Houses of Parliament, the wide slow-flowing Thames, and in the distance the London Eye. Suddenly, there was a ROAD CLOSED sign, and a volunteer held up his hand.

Dad wound down the van window and showed him the passes to say who they were.

'Oh! It's you, Mr Ronaldo! We've been expecting you. Is that your bus an' all?'

Dad nodded.

'Well, come on through.'

It was then that twelve policemen on motorbikes surrounded the van and the

258

bus. Abby laughed and Dad giggled as they were escorted like royalty to Parliament Square. Then, as he switched off the engine, Abby and Dad looked at the scaffold that had been erected as they had specified. Abby felt her heart beat faster. Dad looked at her, excitement dancing in his eyes.

They had set up a marquee on the green for everyone and Abby helped Beryl, Glenys and Violet and the rest off the bus. They had some tea and settled in to wait as Dad and Abby went over their plan. They climbed up on the scaffold to see how high it was. Dad had asked for ten metres, and it was spot on. Then Abby pressed her bag to her a little harder than she usually would in nervousness and thought to herself that it felt a little light. She smiled at Dad and opened it, trying not to panic. She saw her jumper and her water bottle, but there was no book.

Abby's heart dropped. Her face suddenly ashen. Her dad looked at her in concern.

'Abby, what's wrong?'

'The b-b-book,' stammered Abby. 'It's not here . . .'

'What do you mean it's not—'

'It's not here!' shouted Abby. 'I double-, triple-checked . . . Someone must've taken it . . .'

Dad's face fell. 'Where did you last see it?' he asked.

'This morning, outside the care home. It was in my bag, I checked . . .'

Dad was sweating now.

'Josh,' said Abby, 'he was there this morning. Who else could it be?'

Dad pulled out his phone and dialled, his hands shaking.

'Sanjeev! Thank God. We need your help . . .'

Sanjeev put down the phone. Then he turned and walked down the stairs into the shop. Sanjeev, Myra and Josh had just got back from the pier where they'd helped put out the chairs for the public screening. Josh had walked back with them for a quick bite to eat before Sanjeev and Myra were off to London and Josh was going back to oversee the screening.

'Right, young man!' said Sanjeev. 'I'm going to ask you something once, and only once.'

Myra had never seen her dad look so serious. Properly serious. Josh looked worried. Really worried.

'Did you take something that wasn't yours this morning?'

Josh looked at him in confusion.

'Dad, Josh has been with me today,' Myra chipped in.

'I'm sorry, I don't understand,' said Josh.

'Did you take something this morning?' repeated Sanjeev.

Josh shook his head.

'Dad? What's wrong?'

'Something was taken from Abby's bag this morning, a book. And without it the magic can't be done.'

Myra looked at Josh, obviously upset that he might have betrayed them. Josh shook his head.

'It wasn't me, please, I promise . . .' and then he stopped mid-sentence.

'Jasmine was there this morning,' he said. 'I saw her.'

Myra's face fell.' She must've taken it.'

'They need it back and pretty sharpish too,' Sanjeev said.

'They'll be hanging around the pier,' said Josh.

Myra nodded.' Come on. Dad, you pick me up at the promenade in twenty minutes.'

Sanjeev nodded as Josh and Myra ran out the door. Myra led the way to the promenade with Josh trying to keep up beside her. They decided to split up when they reached the pier and look around. Josh said Jasmine and Ella would usually be showing off around the slot machines or hanging around the paddling pool being mean about people. Myra ran off around the slot machines but Jasmine and Ella were nowhere to be found. She was breathing heavily, her chest hurting from running all the way. She rounded the corner once more, thinking she may have missed them, when she heard Josh's voice behind her.

'They're by the paddling pool!'

The paddling pool was a little concrete rectangle that they filled with seawater so that little kids and old women could wet their feet safely. Josh and Myra ran towards it, and sure enough, there was Jasmine, sniggering at some larger lady in her swimming costume. Myra felt her blood boil.

'Oi!' Myra had never said that word in her whole entire life. 'Oi you!' she said again. Jasmine turned to see her, and a smirk came across her face.

Josh came up behind Myra as back-up. Ella made a sour face at him.

'Give it back,' said Myra, her voice even.

'I don't know what you're talking about,' Jasmine replied, her eyebrow arching.

'Give me back the book.'

Jasmine laughed.

'You took my friend,' she said. 'Give him back.'

Myra laughed a genuine laugh.

'I didn't take your friend, he's not a possession.'

'He was my friend . . .'

Josh cleared his throat.

'I want to hang out with Abby and Myra because they are not judgmental, they are not mean. They know who they are, and they rock it in ways that you could never dream of.'

Myra looked at him in shock.

'They're cooler than you. Cooler than you'll ever be.'

Myra had never been called cool in all her life. Jasmine looked at him open-mouthed.

'Now give us back that book or else . . .' said Josh.

'Or else what?' asked Jasmine. 'It doesn't even have

any words in it, it's a pile of rubbish.'

It happened so quickly, Myra almost didn't see it. Josh grabbed Jasmine's bag, and in so doing, Jasmine was knocked off her balance and started to stumble backwards, trying and failing to regain her footing. It seemed to happen in slow motion, her heel, the paddling pool, and backwards she fell with a huge splash until she was sitting on her bum in the middle of the pool with everyone laughing at her. Josh opened her bag, took the book out and gave it to Myra.

'Take it!' he said.

Myra nodded and he winked at her.

'You are cool, Myra, and I wanted to say that I like knitting. Actually, I love it. I also love fashion and make-up and everything. Watching you and Abby have the courage to just be yourselves and follow your dreams has made me want to do the same.'

Myra stood open-mouthed. They smiled at each other.

'Now GO!' he said. 'I'll handle the screening.'

Myra ran to the middle of the promenade where, to her astonishment, her dad was waiting in his leather jacket with his motorbike and sidecar. He held out a helmet for her.

'You got it?'

Myra nodded.

'Quick, get in!'

And with that, she jumped into the sidecar and felt the engine roar. They sped off down the promenade towards the motorway and Myra whooped with laughter at Josh waving wildly as they zoomed past.

CHAPTER THIRTY-TWO

The crowd was gathering. It happened slowly at first, and then the knots of families started getting bigger and bigger, the gaps and spaces between them became less and less. A band had turned up and Jamal and Tony were taking turns to dance with a few of the care-home staff on the grass. Dad and Abby and Linda were sitting stony-faced under the scaffold trying not to panic. Dad had explained to Linda about the book and the colour had drained from her face. They had not told the others except Deepa so as not to panic them.

'Do you think they'll make it?' asked Abby.

'I don't know,' said Dad.

'You'll have to get in costume before long,' said Linda, looking tenser than Abby had ever seen her in her life. Abby went into the marquee to fetch Ta-da as he always seemed to calm everything down when everyone was nervous. She pulled him out of his cage and held him and looked around at everyone. Their joy. Their expectation. Her heart sank.

On the motorway, Sanjeev was breaking every speed record. He and Myra had flown down the roads and were finally nearing London. Myra was grasping the book tightly, determined to get it to Abby. She didn't know what it was. She wouldn't ask any questions. She just knew her friend needed it and that was enough for her. As they approached the outskirts of London, the traffic started to get heavier. Sanjeev had been here several times to get cleaning stock for the shop, so he knew a few shortcuts, but since so many people were making their way into the city to see the magic, almost every road was busy.

At Parliament Square, Deepa buttoned Abby into her costume and Abby thanked her quietly. Then, Linda took a brush and started brushing the bird's nest on Abby's head. They stood quietly for a while, with nothing but the sound of the brush snagging through Abby's hair.

Linda tried to make conversation to soothe both their nerves. 'I haven't done this for you for a long time,' she said.

They both knew what she meant. That was what was so good about them together, there was never a need to explain. Linda hadn't brushed Abby's hair since just after her mother died and she moved in to help. Slowly, after around a year, Abby had learnt to do it for herself, and Linda hadn't needed to do it since. Abby had been thinking about what Lenny said recently, about how Linda and Dad argued like a married couple, and the more she thought about it, the more it kind of made sense to her. Abby knew that Linda would never try and take her mum's place, and she knew Linda loved her, so if Dad were to get married again, he could do a thousand times worse than Linda.

'There,' she said eventually, 'we're done.'

Abby turned around once more. Linda smiled at her.

'Not too shabby, Abby, not too shabby at all. Your mum would be so proud.'

Abby smiled at her and then they heard a small cough.

It was Dad clearing his throat. He looked magnificent this evening. The suit he had changed in to was red but with an orangey hue that made him look like he was on fire. His top hat was also red and shiny with a deep black shiny ribbon to set it off. He was using Mum's magic wand tonight. His special one that she had given him for their wedding. Someone came to take a picture of them, and then Abby snuck a look outside. It was getting noisier and noisier. The film crew had arrived and had set up their cameras in all of the locations and the big screen had gone up so that Abby and Dad could be seen from way back, but it was the crowds that blew her away. Face after face. She didn't know there were so many people in the world. She felt herself shrinking. Her face pale. Dad was looking now too.

'What if they don't get here?' she murmured, feeling sick.

Dad kissed her head and said nothing.

Sanjeev and Myra were almost in Central London. It was then that they screeched to a halt at the barriers. Sanjeev tried to explain that they were friends of the magicians, but the staff were having none of it. They didn't have any proof that they were involved with the magic show. Sanjeev pleaded with them, but more and more volunteers and bystanders started wandering over, wondering what the ruckus was. They were asked to turn back immediately. Myra watched as her dad did what was asked.

'Dad, what are you doing? We can't turn back!' protested Myra.

He winked at her. 'Don't worry, your father's got this.'

'What are you talking about? We can't just give up . . .'

'We're only turning back so we can get a good run-up . . .'

'Run-up?' asked Myra. 'What do you mean?'

'I mean, run-up run-up,' he said. And then, he spun the bike around until it skidded to a stop and revved the engine as if he had the latest sports bike. The motor roared.

'GET OUT OF THE WAY! KEEP CLEAR!' Sanjeev shouted, as the volunteers and bystanders all looked on. Then, they hurriedly scuttled out of the way as they realized what was about to happen.

Myra swallowed hard.

'We're going through the barriers?!'

'Yes, baby!' shouted Dad, pulling his visor down from the top of his helmet and over his eyes. As he did, he pressed the accelerator until the tyres screeched and plumed with smoke, then hurtled towards the barriers sending everyone running for cover.

BANG! The barriers went flying and Sanjeev rode the motorbike like a demon.

'Holy moly, Dad!' Myra cried.

'WaaahOOOOO,' he replied.

Then, they sped their way into the centre of London, zoomed over Westminster Bridge and skidded into Parliament Square where Myra's mum was waiting for them. Sanjeev took off his helmet as Myra's mum ran towards them.

'Oh my God you two!' she shouted. Myra got out of the sidecar and threw off her helmet.

'I have it!' she cried. Myra's mum shouted at her, 'GO! GO!'

Myra ran and just before Deepa turned to go with her, she smiled at her husband and kissed him full force.

'You're so handsome when you're all hero-y.'

Sanjeev looked very bashful and puffed his chest out a bit before following them.

CHAPTER THIRTY-THREE

Parliament Square was full. The band had stopped playing and night was falling, blanketing the city with a soft haze. The city lights were twinkling softly and everyone in the crowd had relaxed a little. Abby and her father had done an interview with the TV station and Abby could've almost cried when she saw Myra run towards her with the book in her hands.

'Here you go,' said Myra, breathing heavily.

'You absolute star!' Dad said, his face beaming. Then he grabbed them both into a group hug.

'Well, it was my dad that was the hero actually,' Myra said, looking back to see her parents making their way through the crowd arm-in-arm.

'Good luck!' Myra said, and smiled broadly at Abby. Abby nodded back and watched as her best friend went to find a place in the crowd with her parents.

The sense of anticipation was almost unbearable now and Dad grabbed Abby by the arms. He steadied his eyes on her.

'Ok, breathe,' he said. 'Are you ready?'

Abby nodded.

'I think so,' she said, her voice tiny as she held the book close.

Then her father looked serious once again. 'Do you trust it, Abby?'

Abby looked lost for a moment.

'Do you trust the magic?' he repeated.

It was then that everything kind of fell into place. In that small tent, with an enormous crowd outside, she could feel nothing but her father and her mother's love all around her. The way the book had come into their lives and let them live again.

'Do you trust yourself? Trust this world?' Dad asked again.

Abby nodded. Her father looked relieved.

'I think you should do the trick by yourself,' he said, 'the whole trick, instead of me.'

Abby was dumbstruck.

'I'll be there to assist you if you need me, but it's your magic. It's your night.'

Abby could hardly speak.

'It'll be brilliant, Abby-cadabra.'

Jamal and Beryl and all the staff from the care home were seated in front of the platform and Myra's mum and dad held her close and were watching as Abby started to climb the scaffold. Linda was holding Lenny's arm and Abby could feel their warmth around her. She looked back at her father who was climbing up behind her and saw an unshakeable faith in his eyes. She turned and climbed higher, felt Dad's footsteps on the rungs below her. Then she stood on the platform and looked down. What she saw took her breath away. It was a sea of people. A sea of faces. Each one looking up. Smiling. A wonderful positivity in the air. There were ripples of applause, an electric anticipation.

'Take it in,' whispered Dad behind her, 'enjoy it.'

There was a microphone to pick up her voice and despite the crowds, the noise and the scale of the event, as she moved to the front of the platform to begin, she felt a lightness. A disappearing into the magic itself. She had known that the book was hers and she didn't hide it this time. She held it in her hands, this gift that she'd been given, and she started speaking.

'Life is short,' she said, 'someone very special taught me that. Life can be hard and unpredictable. Wonderful and joyous too, but we are so distracted with worry, with work, with whatever tomorrow might bring that we forget about today.'

There was a ripple of applause.

'And sometimes, we think too much of the past. It casts a shadow over us and what I have learnt is that we must live for today. For now. We should enjoy the moment. We should treasure every moment because it is golden.'

There was more applause.

'I have grown up in a magical family, I was brought up in the midst of illusions and tricks, but my parents—' Abby felt her voice crack a little – 'my mother and my father showed me the difference between illusions and real magic.'

Abby could feel Dad's presence behind her.

Galvanizing her. Giving her strength. They had not rehearsed this, but the words flowed from deep inside her, from places that were opening up and coming to light.

'My parents showed me that real magic is in the people around us, those who love us.'

At this Glenys looked around her with tears in her eyes.

'Real magic,' continued Abby, 'is kindness, hope, gentleness. It is in standing up for what is right, and being true to yourself. It is about taking every single new day and living every single minute of it. Fully. With your whole heart. And if we do that . . .

. . . then we can stop time . . .'

There was no sound now. Just the upturned faces below her. Everyone waiting with bated breath.

Abby opened her book and looked at the beautiful symbols and letters that had become so precious to her now. It was the last type of spell. She focused and focused and then came the familiar feeling as the ink moved, becoming liquid, and she felt the warmth of the disappearing spell run through her. And the words came . . .

'Tempora verdu . . . tempora verdu . . .'

Abby looked up at Big Ben, one of the most famous clocks in the world, and sure enough, it was fading, becoming translucent.

A gasp of disbelief went up in the crowd and Abby felt her skin tingle.

'Tempora verdu . . .' She concentrated hard and, before the audience's eyes, the bricks became see-through, the dial dulled and the ticking, which had controlled so much of the lives of everyone who stood underneath it, disappeared. People gasped as their watches disappeared in front of their eyes. Those watching the magic on television found the clocks on their mantlepieces and on their walls disappeared too. The clock on the wall of the pier pavilion also vanished. There was nothing there. Nothing. Absolutely nothing. Time had disappeared. There was just now. Without the looming clocks and the watches, they were free from time.

Abby looked up, her cheeks flaming. Her hair shining against her red dress, and then came the roar. The roar of disbelief and cheering. The idea that time had stopped and that they should just enjoy the now. The crowd danced below. They sang. They hugged and some of them called home to tell their loved ones how much they cared for them. There was a sigh of relief, a feeling of living and of being immortal. The joy was palpable, and then Abby felt Dad's hand on her shoulder. The radio stations and the journalists were going crazy, and then, slowly, Abby's concentration waned, and the clock came back, but the moment of its disappearance would last forever. Then, Abby felt a warmth under her fingers, and the book moved out of her hands and flew upwards, glowing like a silver bird. Up and up it flew and then burst into silver confetti that rained onto the crowd below.

Abby turned and Dad held her. The book was gone. They stood, listening to the cheers as the last of the confetti flew around them.

'That was the best thing I have ever seen,' he whispered.

Abby couldn't speak. She just nodded.

'It was wonderful,' came a voice behind them. Abby and Dad looked back in shock. It was Violet.

'How on earth did you get up here?' he asked.

Violet smiled. She tapped the side of her nose. 'Oh, you know.'

Abby looked at Dad puzzled.

'I'm afraid that I have misled you a little. My name is Violet Thardo.'

Abby racked her brains. The name was so familiar. 'The snake lady!' exclaimed Abby.

'Not quite, she was my grandmother,' she said.

Dad's jaw dropped.

'I was worried you might spot me there for a while,' she said, those familiar green eyes twinkling.

'I am the chairwoman of the Magic Triangle. I saw you were doing good work, and so I came to investigate.'

'You weren't just living at the care home?' asked Dad.

'Oh dear me, no,' she said, 'though it was quite the cover, wasn't it?' She smiled.

Then, she opened her handbag and brought out two golden triangle pins. She pinned one onto Dad, and one onto Abby. Then she bowed.

'Welcome to the Magic Triangle,' she said.

Dad almost hit the floor for the second time in a week.

'You have proved that you understand magic, its purpose. Its power. And that although it belongs to us, it is in fact more than us too. You passed the test.'

'Test?' asked Dad.

'Absolutely.' Violet winked. 'Ever wonder what those symbols on the wand your wife left you mean?' She pointed to the wand in Dad's hand now.

Dad was shaking.

'This, my dears,' she whispered, 'is just the beginning.'

Abby looked on in disbelief.

'Now, I don't know about you, but I'd kill for a cup of tea and a slice of Victoria sponge,' she said, and then she disappeared.

Dad looked around. Left. Right. She was nowhere to be seen.

'Oh my God,' said Dad, 'she's goooooood!'

Abby looked at her dad, still almost speechless. The golden triangle on his chest glistening.

It was his turn to be speechless now and he hugged her hard.

CHAPTER THIRTY-FOUR

The dancing lasted into the small hours. Dad and Abby joined in the party and sang and laughed with everyone around them. Then, as the crowd had started to dwindle on Parliament Square, they changed back into their normal clothes and helped Linda and Lenny get everyone back on the coach safely. Tony pulled Dad into a very awkward embrace and told him that he was actually going to bite the bullet and ask Beverley for a date because he was in love with her and had been for around five years. Myra went back on the coach, Sanjeev and Deepa went home on the bike, Sanjeev feeling very rock and roll.

Abby and Dad loaded the old van and slowly made their way home as they had done a thousand times before. Except this time, they had a million-pound cheque in their pockets and two magic triangle pin badges on their T-shirts.

They listened to the road as the miles went by and stopped for chips and lemonade as they were absolutely starving by now. Then, Abby slipped off her shoes and put her feet up on the dashboard and reached for Ta-da, who had enjoyed his first trip into a city. She was stroking him now as the dawn light started breaking on the horizon.

'I've been thinking,' said Dad.

'M-hm?' answered Abby getting sleepy now.

'How'd you feel about repairing the bus, going to see a little of the world like your mum and me planned to?'

Abby looked at him, her eyes widening. 'What about school?'

Dad shrugged. 'What about it? There's always, ahem, homeschooling. I'll tell them you'll be back next spring.'

Abby smiled in disbelief. She ran it though her head.

Myra had Josh now to keep her company until she came back, and perhaps it would do them good.

'It's just that I think we've stood still for far too long,' Dad added, 'and as you know, the big magicians, they always hit a town and then leave.'

Abby laughed at this.

'I'm sure Beverley won't mind keeping my job open . . .'

'You still going to work there?'

'Of course,' he replied. 'They're like family now, and I think there's always room for a little magic on the side.'

Abby smiled.

'So? What do you say?'

'I think it's a splendid idea.'

'I thought you might,' he said.

After they got home, they were both too excited to sleep. They stayed up and went outside to watch the slow turning of the world and a new day appear as if by magic. Dad went to make them tea and they sat in the long grass thinking how beautiful the sky was and how lucky they were.

CHAPTER THIRTY-FIVE

The end of summer had arrived, and even though the tourists were leaving the town, it did not feel despondent like it usually did at this time of year. There was a new energy. Abby and Dad had presented a cheque to the old pier, which had plans to open a stage school for the local children. The town library was getting a new lick of paint, and the care home had begun a mentoring system where young people could come and listen to the life experiences of the residents. Abby and Dad had spent a lovely week having their picture taken for the papers, but now they were ready for another adventure.

Linda still had her clipboard. She was supervising the loading of the bus. Dad had done some repairs and the night before he and Abby had turned the ignition to see what would happen. For the first time in over ten years it roared into life. Abby and Dad had laughed and jumped around at its slow shuddering sounds. This morning, Linda was in charge. They loaded the bus with supplies, enough for a few weeks at least, and as there would be more than just Abby and Dad, Linda had made sure there was extra of everything. Ta-da would come with them, of course, and Lenny was going to look after the pigeons until they came back. Sanjeev and Deepa were going to look after Lenny. Linda had packed her own suitcase and was looking a bit nervous as she'd never been further than London in her life. Abby looked at Linda, who was double-checking her list as she stood outside the bus smoking, when her dad walked by.

'Dad? Linda?'

They both looked at her.

'I just wanted you to know that, you know, if . . . if you want to tell me something then it's alright . . .'

Linda threw down her cigarette in confusion, 'Abby, you're making no sense as usual.'

Abby could feel herself getting hotter. Sweatier.

'What I mean is, if you two are together-together then it's alright by me.'

Linda looked as if she'd been shot.

'Oh my God, I've just been a little bit sick in my mouth,' she gagged. 'Are you serious?'

'Well, it's ok . . .'

'Stop right there,' she said. 'I would rather go out with a gorilla than Ronald here.'

'Thank you, Linda.'

'You're welcome.'

'Seriously? Where on earth did you get that idea from?' Linda asked.

'It's . . . It's just you said you made a great team, that's all.'

'Of course we do,' Linda exclaimed. 'I love you,' she said to Abby, and then poked Dad in the ribs, 'and you, you ugly lump.'

'Again, thank you Linda.'

'But not like that . . . Yuck . . . I am way out of your league, Ronald.'

Abby smiled and then laughed as Linda rolled her eyes at her.

And then, everyone started arriving, everyone who was coming on the adventure and everyone who wasn't.

Linda kissed Lenny proudly on the head and said, 'Behave yourself till I come back.'

Lenny nodded and hugged her.

'And just to clarify, Ronald and I are just friends . . . ok?'

He smiled, 'Thanks, Mum.' Then he turned to Abby, 'I'll look after the pigeons, don't you worry.'

Abby nodded. Myra and Josh were there too and Myra ran straight towards Abby and almost strangled her in a hug. She was beaming about something.

'Glenys has offered to teach me every Saturday – help me make my own collection!'

Abby smiled. 'That's amazing!' She found herself jumping up and down with her.

Sanjeev and Deepa looked at them lovingly.

'I just wanted to tell you before we go to London to see Ishan. He's doing really well,' said Myra.

'That's brilliant,' said Abby smiling.

And then Sanjeev shook Dad's hand. 'And thanks so much for helping us out with Ishan's treatment too.'

Dad smiled warmly, 'It's all for one and one for all around here!' he said smiling.

'Right,' said Dad, 'we all ready to go?'

'One left!' came a voice from behind them. It was Violet in a glorious new hat, dragging a shopping cart behind her. Dad had been expecting her.

'Wait for me.'

Then she sprang up the bus steps as if she were twenty years old.

Abby watched her go. 'This is going to be amazing,' she said.

Myra kissed her cheek. 'Write to me,' she said.

'Of course!' And then Abby jumped onto the bus herself. Linda strapped herself in. Dad jumped into the driving seat and Abby pulled a seatbelt over her. Dad shouted, 'So long, SUCKERS!' and turned the key. Abby's heart stopped. The engine didn't turn over. There was nothing but a whining noise. He tried again. Nothing but a clunk clunk clunk this time.

Abby watched as his shoulders sank.

'Ok, well, this is embarrassing. Everybody off! You're going to have to wait while I fix it. Sorry, folks!'

'Well,' said Violet smiling, 'that's one option . . . or—' and with that she pulled a wand out of her bag.

'We could always do this . . .'

And with a flick of her wand, the engine roared into life. The bus shuddered forward and with that jumped into the air. Everyone outside gasped as it hovered a couple of feet above the ground and then with an almighty . . .

WHOOOOOOOOOOOOOOOOOSH!

. . . they were GONE!

THE END

ABOUT THE AUTHOR

Caryl Lewis is a multi-award-winning Welsh novelist, children's writer, playwright and screenwriter. Her breakthrough novel *Martha, Jac a Sianco* (2004) is widely regarded as a modern classic of Welsh literature, is on the Welsh curriculum, and the film adaptation – with a screenplay by Lewis herself – went on to win six Welsh BAFTAS and the Spirit of the Festival Award at the 2010 Celtic Media Festival. Lewis's other screenwriting work includes BBC/S4C thrillers *Hinterland* and *Hidden*. Lewis is a visiting lecturer in creative writing at Cardiff University, and lives with her family on a farm near Aberystwyth.

ABOUT THE ILLUSTRATOR

George Ermos is an illustrator, maker, and avid reader from England. He works digitally and loves illustrating all things curious and mysterious. He is always trying to incorporate new artiness from the various world cultures he reads about and explores.

'Magic . . . SEED will cast a spell on you'
Frank Cottrell-Boyce

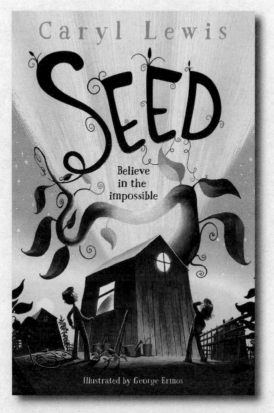

Marty doesn't have much. Unlike his mum, who has
billions of things: newspapers, holey shoes, broken
picture frames – she keeps EVERYTHING. Their house
is almost full to the brim. Marty does his best to look
after her and wonders if anything will ever change.

But on Marty's birthday, Grandad gives him a very
special seed. Grandad hasn't been this excited since
he invented the bum scratcher 2000, or thought he'd
brewed wonder fuel from rhubarb leaves! The seed
grows bigger and bigger, and launches Grandad, Marty
and his best friend Gracie on an impossible, wondrous
adventure fuelled by love, hopes and dreams.